About the Author

A new author who has discovered a love for writing after being in the professional technology world for decades.

Diamonds and Deceit

Jeanne Hall

Diamonds and Deceit

Olympia Publishers
London

www.olympiapublishers.com
OLYMPIA PAPERBACK EDITION

A CIP catalogue record for this title is
available from the British Library.

ISBN: 978-1-80074-337-3

This is a work of fiction.
Names, characters, places and incidents originate from the writer's
imagination. Any resemblance to actual persons, living or dead, is
purely coincidental.

First Published in 2022

Olympia Publishers
Tallis House
2 Tallis Street
London
EC4Y 0AB

Printed in Great Britain

Dedication

This book is dedicated to my two children who are living proof that each generation is better than the one before. Love you two lots and lots like jelly tots. Mum xxx

1

When Billy popped his clogs a few years ago, I was (as usual) left to pick up the pieces. I say as usual because I had picked up the pieces for Billy many times before, in many different countries and at many different times. Picking up the pieces that were broken were always about matters of the heart because Billy had his heart broken so many times, I lost count. You'd think that for a guy that was married and divorced seven times, he might have learnt some stuff along the way but I don't think that ever happened. Slow learner in matters of the heart my dad.

If I had a dollar for every time Billy told me, "That this woman was definitely the one", I probably wouldn't be writing this book because I'd be totally fucking loaded and not in need of another income. Anyway, I never got those dollars so I'm glad you bought my book. Thank you!

Billy was an extremely complex man. Raised by two very beautiful, humble, not-well-educated parents in East Africa — his dad a carpenter and mum a dressmaker — there was not too much money nor many privileges when he grew up. Especially when you were one of five brothers. I think Billy learned a lot growing up in that environment, especially how to lie (to get out of trouble) and certainly how to dream. And boy, could this guy dream. And lie. Fuck, could he lie! He fabricated a life that involved many lives and lifetimes.

You see Billy had so many personalities and so many real and self-created lives that you never really knew which was which. I certainly grew up not being able to clearly determine fact from fantasy (something I still get confused with today and fuck, let's face it, at fifty I should know better).

But I guess when you grow up in such a web of lies and deceit, it's to be expected. To this day I hate liars. Even if there is a whiff of deceit or a white lie, I will generally run a mile from that person, unless I love them to distraction that is. If I love the person, I give way too many chances to them to redeem themselves which of course, is about as healthy as a year-long diet of processed and take-away foods, but hey, that's life right? Until you get to be old enough that you take responsibility for your own actions, it was kind of nice blaming lots of things on Billy.

Let me be clear, he is responsible for a lot of the shit sandwiches I've eaten in this life but at the end of the day, I like to say that without the little guy, I wouldn't be the person I am today. And I kind of like who I am today.

Back to Billy. He was a small man but what he lacked in height, he made up for in attitude and charm. He could be a charismatic son of a B if it suited him. Billy could charm the birds right out of the trees. I remember so many occasions when he made me so mad, I thought I was going to kill the little fucker and then five minutes later, I would be laughing so much, I'd just about be wetting myself.

Sadly, this wasn't always the case. I could also remember being incredibly scared of Billy growing up. Let's be clear here. Dad was a fascinating, complex man. He was also a complete effing lunatic and growing up with him was pretty scary. He had an extremely dark side to him which bordered on the sadistic. He also had a temper that was so volatile and quick that we lived in constant fear. We were always on edge. We never really knew when he would go off his nut, but we certainly knew it was coming. Often. For a little kid, *it, was, terrifying*.

Anyway, let's get back to Billy popping his clogs, shall we? He died a slow, painful death that many would say he deserved. I'd like to agree, but I'm not that kind of person. I don't like it when people suffer, no matter how bad they are. Except for paedophiles, I don't care how long or terrible their suffering is. In fact, the longer the better for paedos. Sorry, I digress.

My immediate problem was writing a eulogy. So as eulogies go, one is meant to honour the deceased. Right? Say nice things. Obviously, you can't stand up in front of the priest, family and friends and say the deceased was an absolute prick and you're thrilled he's dead. Especially when he was your dad. Well, I suppose you can but I guess it would be quite a short service and anyway, seeing I was paying for the funeral, I had to make it nice. Well as nice as funerals go but you get what I'm saying, right? If I was going to be rude about him, I may as well have saved myself ten grand and left him at the morgue. Just saying.

I think eulogies kind of gloss over things. Thank God I had the help of a really nice lady who could translate my words, i.e., "he was a right prick a lot of the time" to "Billy was a rascal and a larrikin" so it got sorted eventually.

Don't get me wrong, I loved that man. I loved the real, raw Billy that perhaps made up 10% of his overall character, The other 90% I was either scared of or angry at. Believe me that 10% was as big as some people's *whole* personality so it was enough for me. And today, when I think of Billy, I only ever think of the 10%. Thank God for Pollyanna syndrome which is a personality trait I definitely did not get from Billy. I don't know where I got it from actually but I remain an eternal optimist.

I don't mean to be morbid here but I thought you guys should read the eulogy. For a few reasons. You can see how fabulous this friend translator of mine was because Billy comes across as super cool in the eulogy. In fact, if I remember correctly, I can remember people who attended the service totally cracking up with memories of Billy as I was reading it. To be honest, I'm not sure if they were cracking up from good memories or just relief that he'd finally carked it. I thought it rude to ask so left it alone.

The second reason to read the eulogy *at the start of a book*, it probably because it does summarise the man and depicts him as a real lad—an all-round nice guy.

Anyway, get through the eulogy and I'll get into a bit more detail on the 10% as well as the 90% of Billy's personality. Be prepared to laugh and cry and imagine living with the little fucker's antics.

2
The Eulogy

"Thank you all for coming to bid my father farewell today.

Thank you also for all the support during this sad time for my family. Dad was known as Bill or Karl but to me, he was just Dad. I would like to outline some of the memories of my dad and talk of some highlights and interesting stories to pad out his character.

My dad was born and raised in Kenya, the middle child of five brothers. Life in Kenya was sometimes hard and harsh with many brutal lessons.

My father developed an active imagination probably to cope with the harsh realities so that he could escape into his own better world.

He was charismatic and he could charm the birds out of the trees. His belief in his own world led him on many escapades around the world.

A few of the more amusing and heart-breaking tales included the ongoing pursuit of the perfect woman which led to several marriages. Oh, how he loved the ladies. Of these many ladies, my mother was his first wife. My sister who cannot be here today was their firstborn. I came along two years later.

My earliest memories are of a fun-filled, crazy childhood. My dad had an amazing laugh and was always up for mischief. We did a lot of camping and fishing together back then. My dad also had a great passion for gambling and we used to get very excited when he went off for an all-night poker game with his mates — mainly because we knew that when they ran out of cash they paid my dad in all kinds of merchandise, so we always had a lot of fun unpacking the station wagon the next morning.

Those fun-filled days changed somewhat when we moved away from our family to South Africa when I was about nine years old. We missed our family, especially Dads parents, Mamma and Pappa. I think that's when our lives as kids changed forever. Shortly after we arrived in South Africa, my parents divorced. Life was truly never the same again.

Many amazing adventures of my dad's money-making schemes and his knack of making (and sadly losing) many fortunes show his heightened innovation and high intelligence.

In my early twenties, and continuing throughout my adulthood, our roles of parent/child somehow were reversed. My dad called me from all corners of the globe to rescue him from another broken heart or from some strife and I always went to him. Depending on where he was, I went by air or by car but I was always "saving" him from something (usually from himself).

I remember flying to London to see if he was okay about three years before he died. We spent two fantastic days together (obviously helped by a few bottles of whiskey and a few zillion cigarettes) and we talked a lot about life. I have very fond memories of that trip.

Other times I would be so mad at him for making me run

around the world to check if he was okay. It didn't matter how angry I got, he would give me that irresistible cheeky grin of his and say, "Oh LuLu, don't be mad, you're here now so let's go to the pub"- and off we went to the pub to sort out his latest heartbreak and problems in his world. My dad's charisma and charm were exceptional and his dramas always tugged at my heart.

My dad had a tremendous capacity to filter out those things in his life that were unpleasant, harsh or ugly. This he did through his adventures, story-telling and living life to the full.

I think he tried to create beauty and love in a loveless and sometimes cruel world. I stand here today as a respected and professionally acknowledged person and I have no doubt that I have followed my dad's self-belief — that is, whatever I set my mind to do I will achieve.

I have learnt from my dad to be an independent, free-thinking person and to view the world as limitless. I also have his ability to be a bit of a dreamer.

My dad's friends and family called him "Makora" which in Swahili means rascal. I think that is a term of endearment more than anything else but still descriptive of his nature.

So Dad, to close this I wish with all my heart that those things that have eluded you all your life, you have now found. That inner peace, happiness and love are now yours.

Thank you for being my dad. Thank you for being tough with us because it taught us how to stand on our own two feet and left us with a legacy that can never be undervalued. Thank you for being the best Dad you knew how to be. Thank you, Dad for ensuring there was never a dull moment in our lives.

I ask only two things: look after my sister and me and your grandchildren, especially my two children — oh, and keep the bar open till I get there.

Okay, Dad, rest in peace and I know that for the rest of my life whenever I reach for the stars, I know you will be holding my hand."

3
His Early Years

Billy's early years in Mombasa were harsh. His family were poor, hard-working people and honest as the day is long. He was the middle child of five brothers and because he had such a smart mouth on him, he often took the blame for many skirmishes. I remember my uncle telling me once that they always sent Billy to the 'frontline' to face their parents, particularly their father's wrath. Billy could, after all, talk his way out of a paper bag. He always was so damn smooth, I often wondered if he could slide uphill.

I think his early years were quite tumultuous but being Billy, he made the most out of every situation. Basically, if he didn't like the real version of his life at the time, he could easily fabricate and dream his way into one he preferred more. Perhaps, that is how he survived the sometimes-harsh conditions, of his formative years.

His dad was an extremely dictatorial and often angry man. I remember once hearing that Billy's oldest brother had been caught smoking when he was about fourteen years old. The punishment for this crime, was to be hung by his ankles, upside down, in an old well filled with rats, with his nose within nibbling distance of said rats. He was suspended for hours like this. Far fucking out. Seriously, I think the punishment was a bit of an overkill myself. Poor bastard was only experimenting with a ciggie, he didn't kill anyone.

Another brother was caught stealing something from someone. I'm not totally clear on the detail of this one, but I do know it was some petty theft. Like he didn't hold up a bank or anything. He probably nicked a cigarette — that was how small the crime was. Anyway, a crime is a crime and the punishment was severe. The brother's hands were wrapped first individually, then together with many layers of newspaper and secured with rope. Then set alight. The words overkill and sadistic ring in my head over this one. I mean let's face it, try doing something like that today and it would be child abuse and you would probably do some time. Sadly, back in those days the father was the head of the family and could rule his wife and children any way he chose. By the way, this kid had third-degree burns from the tips of his fingers to above his elbows.

The interesting part of this level of punishment is I don't think it deterred these five brothers at all from reoffending. They continued to fly their kites quite close to the wires for all of their lives. Some with dire consequences when they became answerable to the law as adults. Totally sad. The sins of the fathers.

So Billy grew up. He was not an academic but he was street-smart and extremely smart-mouthed and he got through his school years. Naturally, he was always in trouble at school, clearly never going to be the head boy but then he was having way too much fun to care about that. By his early teens, he was already ridiculously popular with the girls and let me tell you, his bad-boy image was already totally established by then. A heady mix for the ladies. Note to self: why are women such idiots sometimes? Why do we love the bad boys? Why don't we take the safe bet and hook up with the nice guys? I digress and am going to leave this subject alone, mainly because I personally was that idiot for many years of my life. I guess bad boys are a lot more fun.

Billy was one of them. He took what he wanted, when he wanted, with not a care for the trail of broken hearts (and hymens) he left behind. Don't get me wrong, like all bad boys, he knew how to charm them, he knew how to reel them in and once hooked, how could they ever say no? A bunch of flowers at the right time, a dinner/dance fit for a princess and he was in like flint.

He married none of them of course mainly because he didn't have time. The MauMau war was on suddenly and he enlisted, much to his beautiful, kind mother's dismay. Billy had a sadistic side to him and enlisting was the perfect way to get some of that terrible anger out of him. You see his job was to kill as many MauMau's as he could. Once he killed them, he had to cut off their hands and deliver these hands back to headquarters. For every pair of hands he delivered, he was paid a "treaty". Combined with his anger and sadistic side, he was also the biggest racist I have ever known in my life. He hated black people and that racism just grew to include the rest of the Asian population later in life.

So killing the black MauMau people was fun for him. And he was doing it legally which made it even better. AND being paid for it. Well kill me now because how wrong is that? Anyway, it kept him out of other trouble for a couple of years. The war ended and Billy went home.

He very soon became bored with the women in the town he lived in. My guess is he had had his wicked way with most of them anyway and was looking for, well let's just say, fresh opportunities. The decision to leave Kenya was made for him in the end when he was caught mid-fling with someone else's wife. The husband was hunting him down so Billy embarked on the first of many "gotta leave the country or I'm going to get caught/killed" journeys. He did a runner out of Kenya and ended up in Pretoria, South Africa where he met my mum.

I guess you could say Billy and his brothers did not have a well-rounded, loving family environment to thrive in. His mum was a beautiful soft-hearted woman who just got beaten, literally and figuratively, by her angry husband and would never have had the courage to stand up to her husband during the times he went too far in the punishment of his children.

Funnily enough, his parents remained married for well over sixty years. I adored my grandmother and feared my grandfather. Only when my grandfather was well into his eighties did he soften somewhat, and I grew to love him a little bit then. He was a pretty ferocious old man.

So Billy ran and continued to run and re-invent himself for most of his life. He was never close to his family other than his mum and youngest brother and he kept a good distance between himself and them for most of his life. I often wonder if he thought he was better than them or simply disillusioned by life.

4
Match made in Hell

Do I need to spell out that my mum was a young South African girl who was brought up in a strict, no-bullshit-there-are-rules environment? Raised by a staunch, religious Afrikaans family, she was twenty, lived at home with her parents and had led a ridiculously protected, sheltered life. Her father was an alcoholic which provided a lot of instability in their home, but her mum ruled the house, husband and children with a will of steel. My mum was certainly no woman of the world that's for sure.

She was naïve, young and extremely keen to get out of her parent's house. Perfect storm.

And. In. walks. Billy. Billy. The. Bad. Boy.

Instant attraction naturally. Obviously. Because the good girls like the bad boys, right?

Except this was not Billy as we knew him. This was not the young Kenyan boy Billy with MauMau blood still fresh on his hands that fled Kenya because there were no more virgins or married women that he fancied.

Meet the new Billy. Born in Phoenix, Arizona. Yes, Phoenix, Arizona, United States of America Phoenix. Complete with the natural Billy swagger, but this time with an American accent that is so thick you would actually have no doubt in your mind that you are talking to an actual Yank.

Oh, and he only wore cowboy boots which made him look taller, but more importantly, added to the image that he was indeed an American cowboy.

Billy the Yank owns oil fields in Texas wears cowboy boots and talks with an American accent. Oh, and he is loaded. Somewhere between leaving Kenya and arriving in South Africa, he made a shitload of money from his oil wells in Texas.

Well fuck me, it only took a couple of days to get to Pretoria. It definitely did not take long enough to become a different person. Or did it?

Yes, the Billy transition to a better reality had begun. Because that's normal right? You don't like who you are, your current reality so you morph into someone entirely different. Totally normal.

I have to analyse things. So I have been turning this one round in my mind for decades. Like why an American with oil wells producing dirty, filthy bucket loads of cash? Why not an aristocrat pom or a sheep shearer from New Zealand? Completely and totally needless to state that who fucking knows where that mind went? What can I say? I'm his daughter and doesn't the old saying go the apple doesn't fall too far from the tree? If only. If only I had a tenth of his imagination, hell I would've dreamed up a new fucking universe that only I inhabited.

Right, sorry for the rant. Back to Billy the Yank. Wank.

So he starts to date my mum this American Billy. She falls in love within seconds. Let's face it, Billy is in full charm mode. He is ridiculously handsome, five years older than her, a foreigner and fully cashed up. What's not to fall in love with? The charm works fast and within a few months, she's knocked up with my sister. Go, Billy. You dog you!

So they have to get married because breeding out of wedlock was pretty taboo back in the early sixties. You'd think this is where the shit would hit the fan right? because if my menopause is not totally fucking with my body AND my mind, I'm pretty sure this is where you have to produce birth certificates and other forms of WHO THE FUCK YOU REALLY ARE? I don't know how they did, or if they even produce these documents, but married they were.

I'm going to keep this brief. My mother married Billy fully believing that he was a rich American oil baron. Her family and friends believed it. I only believed it when I read the newspaper article that covered the wedding of the century. No expense was spared because Billy was loaded so naturally, he picked up the tab.

The wedding article in the newspaper reads how this fairy-tale (I'm actually crying with laughter) — young Afrikaner girl meets and falls madly in love with the dashingly handsome, super-rich American oil knob. Sorry, rich American oil baron. It states that my mum will probably not be travelling soon (probably because she's up the duff and would cramp Billy's style anyway — wife, what wife?) but her new husband would continue to return to the United States regularly to check on his oil assets. The article also states that "unfortunately the grooms' parents could not attend the wedding as they were on a worldwide cruise to celebrate the latest oil discovery". In fact, his brothers couldn't attend either because they were clearly required at the oil fucking refinery in America. You and I both know the real story was that his family were dirt poor back in Kenya just trying to survive, and of course, they were trying to cover up his tracks in case the husband of the woman he was banging before he left might find him and cut his balls off.

True story people and if nothing else, I hope you are triple careful when meeting new people from now on because let me tell you, all may not be as it appears. Be warned, look before you bloody leap ☺ .

I am still totally puzzled as to how the legal aspects of this marriage were actually rubber-stamped. My parents got married on Boxing Day with Mum complete with a bun in the oven, so I'm safely assuming there was some haste to tie the knot to keep everyone's dignity intact. Plus, there were a few holidays thrown in like Christmas Day. But I draw the only real conclusion I can: there was probably an envelope full of cash handed to the courts and the church to ensure no questions were asked.

Catch me if you fucking can, why don't you?

5
Wedded Bliss

And so, the fairy tale begins. Not so much a fairy tale, but a tale indeed. My sister popped out a couple of months after the wedding and Billy was so disappointed because he wanted a son. Can you imagine his incredible disappointment two years later when I came along?!

Correct me if I am wrong but why would you want a son anyway? What, exactly, did you want him to inherit from you, Billy? Snort. Sorry, I just snorted my wine through my nose. What, exactly, do you want to teach him about life? What possible facts of life would you wish to transfer to this son I ask because believe me, the ones I was taught did me no fucking good. What-so-fucking-ever. This mystery will never be solved, not by me anyway. People should actually be means tested, not financially, but they should have their intelligence tested *prior* to having children, don't you think? I mean, seriously, there are just too many fucktards in the world already, right?

Just saying.

The marriage probably lasted less than a year but they managed to keep it together for sixteen more. I used to question why my mother put up with this shocking behaviour but I don't do that any more. After all, how many times have I fucked up in my fifty years and put up with way more than I should have? Sins of the fathers. And probably many mothers, but this book is about Billy so for now it's the fathers.

Needless to say, it didn't take my mother long to figure out she had married a fake. He lost the American accent as soon as they moved away from Pretoria, away from her family and friends and the ugly truth reared its ugly head.

Billy became an accountant, a no-proof-of-study-required-accountant. Somehow, he got away with being an accountant for decades and no one bothered to check his credentials. There was definitely no framed university graduation certificate hanging in his study at home, no certified document from the Chartered Accountants Society, fuck all. But my God, if Billy told you he was an accountant, then he was a goddamned accountant, right?

Billy worked a series of jobs in and around Pretoria and then presumably got bored with the jobs and the wives of the people he worked with. Oh yes, he was still spreading his seed far and wide. Billy the stud never stopped proving what a fine specimen of manhood he was and believe me, his dick ruled his entire life. More about his dick later.

Sorry, I know that as his daughter, I should know nothing about his dick, but I do. Sadly. Let me be clear here: I have no personal relationship with his dick—to the best of my knowledge I cannot add paedo to his list of issues but due to a series of events, I have first-hand knowledge about his appendage. Keep reading, I'll get to that part. For those ladies who like a large one, Billy was definitely your man. What he lacked in height, blah blah blah.

The "accountant" and my mum moved to South West Africa and the next chapter of 'catch me if you can' began.

6
Diamond Smuggling

The accountant, my mum and my older sister who was only a few months old moved to Swakopmund in South West Africa (now known as Namibia) to enable Billy to work on a diamond mine. As. The. Accountant. I laugh as I type these words. My mother was not happy in Swakopmund. She had a baby daughter to look after and was married to a serial liar/cheater so she had enough to deal with. Especially with no friends or family nearby.

I think this is when she had her first affair. Now let me tell you this was an extremely brave thing to do on my mother's part. Billy was old-fashioned that way and he firmly believed that what was his, was his alone. Totally. Fucking. Hilarious. Especially when you consider he could never, ever keep his pants zipped up and be faithful to any woman. Believe me, if there was a whiff of the bearded clam available, Billy was in like flint and if there wasn't a whiff of it, he made damn sure he found some availability, even if he had to pay for it. Ewww, dirty bastard.

Sorry to be so crass but I am trying to demonstrate here that he was a total love rat. As I mentioned before, Billy's dick ruled his life. If there was a snatch up for grabs, Billy was there like a bear.

I am led to believe that I am the result of that indiscretion of my mother's and I certainly fucking hope so. It would explain a lot of things anyway. But nothing has ever been proven so at this point we will keep going with the notion that I'm Billy's daughter. It is who I have always been and there are too many things that point to this which we won't go into right now. Perhaps one day if I write another book but not now. I prefer to believe it was just my mum talking up a storm when she gets on the piss.

All I can say is that the guy that porked my mother *while* she was married to Billy is an extremely brave man because if Billy had an inkling about it, he would have killed the dude. Billy did not like sharing and really, you would have had to be extremely stupid to make him angry. He had a temper the likes of which I have never experienced since.

So my mum just had to get on with life and deal with stuff to enable Billy to commence his work at the Diamond Mine. The Diamond Mine was real and Billy had a real job there. He was the Accountant God bless him. This is not like the Oil wells in Texas, this is real life for now, with a twist.

I'm going to go out on a limb here and assume you're not silly enough to believe that this would be enough for Billy. A good stable job, a nice little growing family, food on the table and all that shit. And Billy would be content. And pigs will fly. And again, I laugh as I type because naturally, Billy was bored.

So he spent his days figuring out how he could make a lot of money. Quickly. Always scheming. He befriended the mine manager, the Catholic priest and the pilot and started dreaming and concocting the next grand plan. The mine manager was simply an ally but the other three were clearly going to do something that was not ethical. Or legal.

They devised their grand plan. The mine was producing a bucket-load of diamonds and Billy was one of those people who thought that it was wrong that he should be a good upstanding citizen and go to work and earn a wage like everyone else. Definitely not that life for my dad and he felt totally justified in his thinking that he deserved as many diamonds as he wished to have. Working nine to five was for peasants, not for Billy. Billy, who, funnily enough, *was* a peasant. Or certainly from peasant stock but he had grand plans for himself, always wanting more.

At some point, these three chops came up with a plan to steal diamonds. A lot of diamonds. The plan was perfect. After all, South West Africa is home to many snakes. Far too many for my liking anyway. However, in this instance, snakes were going to turn their dreams into reality. Lots-of-diamonds-for-free reality. The snakes were critical in removing the diamonds from the mine because who would ever suspect a snake of transporting diamonds as it slithers through the boundary fence?

Totally fool proof. Billy, the criminal mastermind, figured out that if they filled a pouch full of diamonds, made sure the snake noshed the bulging pouch by inserting it into a rat carcass, then they'd be home and free. The snake would simply slither through the fence to freedom or so it thought. Once it reached the other side, it was, of course, sliced open to enable the removal of the pouch. Fortunes were about to be made. Genius.

They say the simple ideas often take off. This was one of them. It worked for a long time. Once the snake exited the mine, one of the other two conspirators were on standby to catch the snake and retrieve the diamonds. Simple really. And no one suspected anything for a long time. These three galahs thought they were the smartest diamond smugglers of all time. Their plan had worked.

Until it didn't.

Fate stepped in and by fate, I mean the mine bosses were starting to get suspicious. Clearly, things weren't adding up on the balance sheet which makes me laugh like the proverbial drain when you think about who was in charge of the balance sheet. No one really knew what was going on but they did know that the numbers weren't adding up and they were asking questions of the accountant.

The accountant was getting a fair bit of heat so he decided they would do one last snake haul and then cease their thieving activities for a while until the dust settled down. Very. Bad. Decision. Being the greedy buggers they were, they didn't know that things were about to take a very bad turn.

The final snake was locked and loaded and on his slithery way to "freedom" when suddenly there was a fair amount of shouting and screaming out the front of the mine. Oh dear, it was mating season for the snakes and they were out in force to find their shagging partners and oh fuck, which one has the diamonds in his belly?

There were only three culprits who were more terrified of *not* finding the right snake than they were of the actual, extremely aggressive snakes. It was mayhem. This was a big haul so they were frantic to find their snake. Billy had, by this time, left the comfort of his airconditioned office and was out the front with everyone else.

The security guards were trying to move the snakes on, but to no avail and finally had to start shooting the writhing, wriggling snakes. Apparently, snakes are quite dangerous during the mating season: a sort of one-eyed (snort) view to get what they want. I would have thought Billy, of all people, would understand that these snakes just wanted to root. I'm sure he did but he had diamonds on his mind.

As luck would have it, Billy's snake got shot and in a one in fifty-billion-trillion-zillion chance, it got shot in the right spot. Right into a pouch of diamonds. Diamonds. Fucking. Everywhere. The air lit up with the millions of colours from the diamonds flying through the air. And Billy and his two mates standing open-mouthed, cursing like sailors about the loss of "their" diamonds. To put it mildly, it didn't take a rocket scientist to figure out who the guilty parties were.

They were arrested and it went to trial. The three of them were looking at, at least twenty years in jail. Each. Billy would probably get more because he had cooked the books in addition to being the mastermind behind the project. The other two were just accessories really. Swakopmund was a small mining town with not much in the way of fancy courthouses and lawyers. I believe at that point there were only ever two cops in the town and they were drinking buddies with my dad.

They got bail at some point presumably because it wasn't murder. It was more a white-collar crime of theft and fraud. Of millions and millions of dollars in diamonds.

My mother got a quick induction then, as to what was to become the first of many runners they would do during their blissful sixteen-year marriage. She was harshly introduced to leaving town in the middle of the night. Quietly. Don't ask any fucking questions woman, pack up the kid and the car when it gets dark while Billy has a bit of shuteye for the long drive that was ahead of them. She had to wake him at eleven p.m. and they would be off.

Naturally, she did as she was told. She was petrified of my dad in those early years and would never dare argue the toss with him. By midnight they were gone. The journey lasted for months as they ducked and dived and hid in small towns in South West Africa, then ran the border into South Africa and kept moving. Mum wasn't allowed to contact family or friends because they were, well, on the run.

Eventually, they ended up in Durban and managed to board a ship to Australia. What better place I say? Didn't Australia's roots start as a penal colony full of convicts? Great choice Billy. Fucking bravo. He'd got away with it, or so he thought at the time anyway.

He was chuckling like a psycho, no doubt when they were on the open water and he was a free man. I use this term loosely as I believe Billy was never really free. He was always trapped inside his own self-created prison because of all his wrongdoing and the web of lies and deceit he never stopped creating for himself and those around him.

Anyway, back to the ocean journey. He was unbelievably proud of himself, laughing crazily at how clever he was. Not only had he escaped a prison sentence but he was also the custodian of hundreds and hundreds of diamonds. Yep, you'd better believe it, he had screwed his mates over too.

I can't even begin to think what was going through my mother's mind at this time but it can't have been good.

A couple of years later, Billy heard that his two partners-in-crime had been convicted and sentenced to eight and twelve years in prison respectively. I am blown away that the priest got a lesser sentence than the pilot. Makes me think that somehow the Catholic Church has always been rotten to the core because this still doesn't seem fair. Or maybe the priest really had connections to the Big Guy who helped him out? And maybe those pigs do fly.

Billy laughed for weeks when he heard his mates were in jail. Seriously, he laughed. It made him even prouder of himself because he hadn't been caught, you see? It made him feel superior and smarter than everyone else and of course, he had no conscience whatsoever. He must have missed that gene because he felt total fucking rocks for his mates. He just thought they were stupid to have been caught.

If he knew what was to happen many years later, he might not have been so smug. He might even have hung onto a few of the precious diamonds to return to them once they had done their time. But not our Billy. Billy was all about Billy.

I remember when I was about twenty-six, I got the first of many frantic calls from Billy. Well, not so much Billy as the hospital that he'd been admitted to. He couldn't speak. The doctor who called me said he was in a terrible way, so I got in my car and raced to the hospital to see him. We were back in South Africa at that stage and we all lived in Johannesburg, but not together. Billy had been beaten up so badly that the specialists at the hospital were quite sure he would not recover. Clearly, they did not know Billy.

I was pretty devastated and sat vigil at his bedside for many weeks. I think he was in between marriages at that time so I was the only one visiting anyway. Well, what can I say, he healed and he survived and was as normal (and again I use this term very loosely) as before the beating. So as much as

33

the specialists predicted he may end up disabled or with brain damage, he actually came out the same as he was before. I mean there was brain damage before the accident, right? The man was not wired right anyway so I don't think the brain damage worried me as much as the disabled part. And if I know Billy, he would rather have been dead than disabled but his major concern would have been any damage to his looks. Or his dick. As I said before, he was a very vain man.

It took me a long time to get the truth out of him. The boys from South West Africa had not forgotten him. They did their time behind bars and then the pilot came looking for him. Presumably, the priest being a Man of God, could not partake in revenge. Perhaps God only forgives theft and fraud I assume?!

The pilot brought some big friends with him when he came to retrieve his third of the diamonds. When Billy finally convinced him there were none to retrieve, I think the conversation got a little heated. And physical. Remember Billy was a small man and they beat the bejesus out of him. He didn't stand a chance. Or so we all thought, incorrectly. I'm pretty sure they meant to kill the little guy and if Billy were an honest man, he would've agreed with me.

Catch me if you fucking can—well they got him this time and nearly killed him but it would take a lot more than a violent beating to stop this little fucker.

7
Then Along came Moi

My mother was violently ill on the sea journey and soon it became apparent why. A few months after the ship docked in Perth, I entered the world to a loving mother and a complete nutter of a father who wished I were a boy.

I used to wonder why the dice were rolled this way for me.

Why couldn't I have had the perfect family? Normal home, loving parents who adored me other and all that mushy stuff? Then I think, *dry your eyes, boo-fucking-hoo*. Clearly, it would take a strong, amazing person to deal with Billy for decades and I guess I was *it*. I particularly like the strong and amazing part, lol! Anyhoo, I did get through it without having too many mental issues and psych bills. Don't get me wrong, I've read every self-help book ever written, but there is nothing that describes nor solves my particular issues so I'm kind of fucked. Unless someone writes a book called *Growing up with a sadistic conman and how to recover*, I guess I'm permanently screwed.

We remained in Perth for a few years. By this time, Billy didn't have too many secrets from my mother any more so I think they shipped in his parents from Kenya along with a couple of brothers. For someone who was not really close to his family and didn't really have a heart unless it served his own purposes, this was probably a surprising act of generosity on his part. Billy could actually be generous to a fault. If it suited him or if he was going to benefit somehow from the generosity, that is. I think more than likely, he probably wanted to get his parents out of Kenya so they couldn't answer any questions regarding his whereabouts and character if the brass happened to call round. Or if the pilot decided to swing by and teach him another lesson through his parents maybe.

It came as no surprise to my mum that his parents were not American, nor had they ever set foot in America. Ever. In fact, I laugh about this one often. In my dad's entire seventy-four years on this earth, *he* never set foot on American soil either. He must have managed those oil wells remotely. Hysterically laughing now. Sorry, I digress: back to Perth we go.

The half dozen or so years I spent growing up in Perth were the most "normal" years of my formative life. I have the most amazing fond memories of that period of my childhood, perhaps because they were the *only* years of my childhood. Once we left that secure hub of the family, I grew up very fast and by the time I was seven or eight, the roles were reversed where I was suddenly the parent and my dad was the child. I had grandparents who doted on me, parents who were trying to be as normal as possible, cousins whom I adored, a few weird uncles and their fabulous wives. My aunts remain some of my favourite people today although I still have no idea why they married into that family.

My sister, cousins and I used to walk to the local Catholic convent to go to school and we had the best Sunday lunch gatherings and family fun ever. Billy, his dad and brothers always got a bit loud and vocal and the odd fight or two broke out, but I was too young to pay any attention. I remember the best Christmases ever, a huge tree at my grandparents' house, so many presents. The best presents were the ones my grandparents used to make for us. We got canvas deckchairs from my carpenter grandfather and home-made matching dresses for my sisters and female cousin from my granny. And the food was always amazing. My grandparents actually originated from the Seychelles Islands (not America ☺), so there was a bit of French in a lot of the foods we ate, oh and a lot of curries. My dad could eat those tiny, arse-clenching red devil chillies on their own and he loved a hot curry. Every day. If my mother wouldn't make curry, he went to his mother's for dinner, whilst cursing my mother for not cooking "real" food, i.e. curries every night. Billy also believed he had a fine understanding of the French language and I thought he was amazing when he started speaking it. It wasn't until years later when I could speak French, I realised what a fuckwit he was because he knew a few words and made the rest up in true Billy style. Like all the things he bullshitted about, he was always eventually busted.

As mentioned in the eulogy, my dad loved to gamble. Not really surprising I suppose, considering he lived his whole life on pot luck. Some of my best years as a little girl were spent unpacking the family station wagon after a big night of cards. Naturally, my dad was a superb cheat at everything, including cards so no one stood a chance. God knows why they all kept playing. Billy fleeced them all, every single time and when they ran out of cash, he would make them open up their delis or electrical shops and take whatever goods he fancied in lieu of payment. The full station wagon returning home at dawn was like a lucky dip to my mum, my sister and me, totally loaded with goodies. Billy was our hero, even though he had driven home completely arseholes and passed out the minute he walked through the front door.

Do I need to mention here that a few enemies were being created? Fleece people long enough and they're going to come after you.

Billy was working as an "accountant" at a prestigious finance firm for those few years in Perth. Isn't it hilarious that a firm of *qualified and certified* chartered accountants, a really professional and well-known outfit did not ask him for proof of competency or degree or even, for fuck sakes, references? I can assure you if he was an accountant, I am a fucking astronaut.

Luck was clearly on Billy's side back in the mid-to-late sixties as there was no internet and no connected, globalised world or he might not have worked there as long as he did, or even at all. Anyway, he worked there long enough to move a few hundred thousand to his personal accounts. Did I mention how smart and conniving he was? He didn't leave for this reason though. In fact, I don't think they ever discovered the missing money and if they did at some point, he would have been long gone.

He was actually fired for, wait for it, yet again, he got caught banging one of the partner's wives in the boardroom. I think I've already mentioned his dick ruled his life. Some might say ruined.

So we were on the move again, me for the first time. The partner of the company was going to kill the little fucker so we didn't have much choice. Anyway, if he didn't kill Billy, I am sure there would have been a few more in the queue to teach him some manners. Personally, I think Billy could not have cared less. He totally believed he was untouchable and totally invincible.

8
Two more years Down Under

I think I was about five when we did the midnight runner. We crossed the almighty Nullabor a couple of times to buy time while Billy decided whether it was safe enough to remain in Western Australia or to head to the East Coast to Melbourne or Sydney.

Eventually, we ended up in the far north of Western Australia in a town called Marble Bar. I think this was because Sydney and Melbourne were large cities and Billy liked to be the big fish in a small pond, not the other way round.

Marble. Fucking. Bar. Google it. Even as I child I thought we had landed in hell. One of the things Marble Bar was known as was the hottest town in the world — 100 consecutive days of fifty plus degrees Celsius was the norm. It might drop to forty-nine for a few days before day one kicked off again to start another 100-day record. *It was a shithole*.

Flies, snakes and frogs are pretty much all I can remember of Marble Bar combined with the stifling heat. It was also probably one of the remotest towns on earth so I figure Billy thought he would be able to lie low there for a while. After all, you'd have to be nuts to go all the way to Marble Bar to find someone who had slept with your wife or stolen from you at cards surely? The journey alone would not have been worth it, believe me.

Did I mention my dad was the biggest racist on the planet? Well, guess what? Marble Bar was also mostly aboriginals. It drove him nuts. When he wasn't ranting and raving at my mother or us, he was ranting about the aboriginals. He was always ranting back in those days so I didn't pay much attention to the detail. I just knew he was going off again and laid low.

The shit hit the fan one day when my sister brought home one of the said indigenous people from school. They were little seven-year-old friends for goodness' sake. Anyway, everything was going really well during the afternoon. Mum was at home and we baked cakes and biscuits and played games and all was just fine. Until Billy came home from work. Said dark seven-year-old was forcibly removed from our house and all hell broke loose. Billy was furious and screaming to anyone that would listen, that he would not tolerate &<%$& in his house. I didn't know there were so many rude names for dark people until that day so I wasn't clear on what he was carrying on about. I think he decided that night that we were to leave Marble Bar as soon as he could clear his desk at work. And yes, you guessed it, he was an accountant at the local mine. My mother was told to start packing; in a week we would be gone.

The next day we all realised that might not be a bad thing. Word had spread and I reckon we were all going to be lynched or our house set on fire in the middle of the night with us in it. That little dark girl had a loving, *large* family and they were not going to tolerate this from a little "white" guy who was, in fact, almost as dark as them.

Billy had made his mark yet again but this time our form of transport out was not in the station wagon doing a midnight runner. This time it turned into a helicopter. A Royal Flying Doctor helicopter.

By some miracle, the guys at the mine had put on a farewell party for my dad and we were all invited. It was at a house a few kilometres from our house so we all piled in the trusty station wagon and off we went. Apparently, it was a great party. Then we went home. I was sitting in the middle front seat of the station wagon between my parents when the shit hit the fan again.

A guy was standing on the side of the road with an axe. My dad knew him as he worked with him on the mine. Paul was a little on the slow side and spoke with a stutter and my dad, being the compassionate, kind guy he is (not), used to tease him mercilessly at work. Billy called him all sorts of colourful names and even started stuttering himself in, I would say sympathy but my dad didn't have a sympathetic bone in his body so it was just to take the piss. Billy always laughed himself stupid when the guy got all upset. It makes me quite sad to think of this as I would never dream of doing this to anyone. Thank fuck I didn't inherit that nasty gene. It's a genuinely sickening human trait to mock someone less fortunate than yourself, but Billy couldn't care less.

Anyway, payback is a bastard.

Billy was pissed as a newt as usual and stopped next to Paul to ask him what he was doing up this late and standing on the side of the road with an axe. Reasonable questions we thought, but then we did not know the details of their relationship and how much Billy paid out on him.

Before Billy could utter another word, Paul raised the

axe and struck the windscreen really hard. Hard enough to go through the windscreen and slice Billy's head open. He was pretty much scalped. At the same time as the axe sliced through Billy's forehead, his foot hit the accelerator and we shot off. Probably not a bad thing if the guy's intent was to do a mass murder job. Obviously, my mum thought my dad was dead and was quite hysterical (not sure from joy or sadness); we were all covered in blood and probably a tad nervous that the man with the axe was coming to finish us all off.

As Billy fell into a state of unconsciousness, his foot jammed hard on the accelerator and the station wagon took off. We were heading straight towards a massive iron or wall or a very deep ravine depending on which way the steering wheel went. We were dead either way. My mum was frantically trying to control the car from the passenger seat (back seat driver gone too far?) but couldn't budge my dad's leg from the accelerator. By some sheer miracle, she did manage to wrench the keys from the ignition and we came to a stop. About three metres from hard, solid rock and the steepest ravine. Either would have meant death for all of us, including Billy. Not even he would have survived that. We were all alive, covered in my dad's blood.

It gets a bit blurry here. I remember ambulances and volunteer workers and lots of others around the car. Billy was airlifted to a hospital in Perth and we were taken under the wings of lots of lovely volunteers and adults. I do remember sitting in the bath and the water was dark red. It took a few goes to get all the blood out of my hair apparently. My mum, my sister and I were badly shaken but no worse for wear.

Billy. Not so much. He had several emergency surgeries

to keep his brain from falling out, another to insert a titanium forehead/skull as all the bones in the top of his skull were shattered and then finally had his forehead reattached. He lived. I fucking kid you not. How many lives did this man have? Billy spent many months in hospital recovering.

Paul went to jail for aggravated assault with the intent to murder. Poor bastard. The justice system is often not fair. Some would say Billy deserved everything he got.

9
Norseman

So needless to say, Billy made a full recovery. That is to say no *further* brain damage. The guy was already not wired right, to begin with. right? Anyhoo, there was no permanent change to the old Billy after he received his titanium skull.

Clearly, it would have been foolish to return to Marble Bar. The queue of people who disliked Billy was getting longer and would continue to get longer for the rest of his life.

Norseman. Another shithole. Dad worked at a gold mine as the — wait for it — the accountant and mum took on a job as a nurse at the local hospital. We seemed reasonably stable for a short while. Billy was short of money, who knows why, so he got us all an evening job. I was about seven at the time and my sister nine when we started cleaning the four-storey office block at night. My job was to empty and wash out all the ashtrays on all the desks; my sister emptied the bins; mum vacuumed and Billy of course… well… *supervised*. The dog. We'd get home around eleven p.m. and go to bed. Naturally, Billy collected the paycheque. Where were the child labour laws when you needed them?

We had chickens in our back yard. They weren't pets. Remember that sadistic streak I spoke of in Billy? I didn't eat eggs for years after Billy specifically showed me where they come from and told me, over and over, that I am eating something that came out of an animal's bum. Surprised I eat eggs now, or chicken for that matter. I remember him being in a very festive mood almost happy for once. I soon found out why.

Billy had a little Sunday afternoon fun planned and decided he was going to kill a chicken for Sunday roast. But we all had to watch him do it because then we could see what a man he was and how clever he was. And need even more counselling for the rest of our lives.

So we watched. Poor chook. He was placed on a block of wood and farmer Billy got into position with one foot next to said chicken's neck on the block. He half-sliced the chicken's neck off and almost fully sliced his foot off. Fuck me, so the chicken is running around the yard with blood spurting out of his neck hole and my dad jumping around on one foot with the other one hanging on by a tendon. Or a miracle. Blood spurting everywhere.

Family fun day in our household. Bag of laughs in our house. Long story short, the chicken killer got carted off to the hospital, and the chicken eventually died. Probably because it didn't have a head. We ended up having toast for dinner and Billy got to keep his foot. He spent a couple of nights in the hospital and survived. I think I'm still traumatised.

I often wondered what other families do on Sundays. Surely the same as us?

At some point, Billy decided his two daughters were in the way and cramping his style. You know his style of drinking himself into a coma, gambling, womanising. That style. All class, our Billy. So we were shipped off to boarding school a hundred kilometres away in a town called Coolgardie. As termly boarders. I kid you not. An hour's drive from home and we were only allowed to go home *one weekend in every term*. Yes, that's right, we went home for two days every ten to twelve weeks and we counted our blessings because we were allowed to spend the holidays at home too. It was a true blessing to be raised in such a close, loving family. We were not insecure at all as we knew how much our dad and mum loved us. Not. Mum did but she was never going to argue the toss with her husband. I remember missing the dogs the most.

So convent life continued for about eighteen months and then we headed back to Perth. I think Billy's gambling buddies didn't want to be robbed any more and he had screwed all the women in Norseman, so it was time to go. At least this time, we weren't run out of town but I'm pretty sure no one was sad to see us leave. Apart from our little friends at school, I think. But no one was sad to see Billy go. There was certainly no farewell party.

10
Short stop in Perth

Then we spent about three months in Perth getting stuff in order so we could leave again. Some of Billy's frenemies heard we were back and naturally wanted a piece of him so we had to lie low. We couldn't even go to school. We were ordered to stay indoors at our grandparents' home.

It was a pretty boring three months but good that we got to spend a lot of time with our family. If we had known what was to come next, we would have probably enjoyed it a lot more. I think this was the last time we really knew we belonged somewhere.

Obviously, there were a few incidents. You weren't Billy's daughter without knowing that life would never be smooth sailing. There would always be dramas.

After a lot of nagging (and complete secrecy from my dad), my mother finally agreed to let me cut off my below-the-bum long hair to a short, cropped cute style. I loved my new do. Billy didn't. A full-blown tantrum erupted once he noticed (after being home for about three hours without noticing) and I was sent to my room. I went there in tears. I heard him screaming at my mum, saying that if he wanted a boy, he would've had one. Looking back, I laugh because he never had a boy and it was (in his eyes), his greatest failing. After all, if you didn't have a boy, you weren't a real man, right?

Anyway, to add to my insecurities, he then started calling me "son" from then on and referred to my penis for laughs. Sick puppy.

The partner from the law firm looked us up shortly after we returned to Perth. There was much screaming on the front lawn of my grandparents' house and to my horror, my dad was yelling at the partner telling him that his wife was a dud lay anyway and he (the partner) could "keep her". What a bastard. Talking about rubbing the poor guy's nose in it. The partner didn't like it much either and the next day, Billy came home very much the worse for wear. The partner had obviously paid some thugs to give him a damn good hiding. Bravo, I say.

Billy ranted and raved and said hideous things like, "If it's got tits or wheels, it's bound to give problems," and it was absolutely no fault of his that the shag had taken place. Something about loose women. Let's be clear, nothing was *ever* Billy's fault. His dick continued to rule his life.

11
Next stop — Back to Africa

So off we went to South Africa. I guess Billy thought most of his past would have been forgotten by now as it was ten years since they had left. Plus, he had a brother over there that he wanted to see.

We ended up in a town called Empangeni, about 250 clicks north of Durban. Billy was not a big city guy. I mentioned before he was better at being the big fish in the small pond.

We were enrolled in the convent but allowed to stay at home this time. We went to school as dailies. I think I would have preferred going straight in as a boarder. That way, I could have missed the unravelling of my parents' marriage. Billy drank heavily and continued to screw everything that had a pulse. My mother collected a diamond for every time she caught her husband cheating. The diamonds got bigger and more beautiful each time. I guess the size and quality were determined by the depth of the unfaithfulness.

I'm not sure why mum stayed, to be honest. His patterns never changed over the years but as the drinking intensified, so did his appalling behaviour.

Mum always copped it. Don't get me wrong, she was no angel either, but he was an absolute tyrant. Naturally, he accused her of cheating. You know the old saying: when you're guilty you always try to pin your bad behaviour on someone else. The screaming matches every night were a shocker. They fought non-stop. About everything.

I mentioned before how much Billy liked curries. I actually think there was a bit of mixed blood in our family and this was confirmed many years later when we visited my gran back in Australia. My cousin and I stumbled across a very old suitcase full of family photos and yep, you guessed it, there was definitely brethren in there that weren't all white. Hilarious really, when you think how much of a racist he was.

Anyway, I digress. Let's get back to the curries. Billy liked to eat curry every day, for breakfast, lunch and dinner and the rest of the family had to comply. We were little kids and would have preferred a mac-shit every now and again, but this was not allowed. One night mum decided to hell with cooking and brought home KFC.

We thought it was Christmas. She had just finished dishing up (Billy would never eat out of a packet. We had to eat off plates at the table listening to him carrying on like a chop every night) when Billy strutted in. Full of piss as usual and deceptively looking quite happy. Billy's mood swings could rotate in split seconds. You were never complacent, even as a child, because one minute he would be laughing his head off and the next, there was no end to the level of his anger.

The next second, we heard, "F……g take-away, where the f…k is my curry, woman?" and all hell broke loose. With one sweep of his arm, all the food, plates and all, were spread all over the kitchen floor with Billy storming to the lounge screaming that he wasn't eating this shit. My sister and I were so looking forward to eating that shit that we ended up sitting on the kitchen floor, digging through the broken crockery and glass shards and eating it anyway. With the dogs. Friday family fun night yet again. Surely my mum should've realised by now that if it wasn't Billy's way, it wasn't going to happen? Ah, such fabulous childhood memories. Warms the cockles of the heart.

We lived in a beautiful house in Empangeni. It was like a large doll's house with three large A-frames across three levels. I remember there were many parties in that house with both my parents drinking themselves into a coma and putting on the "we are such a happy family" bullshit. I loved those evenings because even I believed for a short time that we were that happy family. It lasted until the guests left, of course. Then all hell broke loose again, with Billy accusing my mum of flirting with his mates or the food was shit, or she wasn't quick enough to bring him another drink.

The screaming started. We would be in bed by this stage but were always woken by the screaming and glasses shattering and things being thrown around. My sister was the smart one as she stayed in her room, but I was always worried he'd kill my mum so I would get up and listen in for hours and hours until things quietened down and he passed out. Once I knew my mum was okay, I'd creep back to bed and go to sleep to the sound of her sobbing her heart out. If only the guests could see this post-party version of the Brady Bunch now.

I remember sitting on the staircase one night while they were screaming at each other upstairs in their room. My dad could be pretty violent and I remember many times when he had my mum backed up against the wall with his hands around her throat, screaming at her that she was lucky to be alive and married to him. Lucky indeed, lol! If only my mum had learnt not to answer back, these fights could have ended a lot sooner but I can only imagine her hurt and frustration. She was married to a narcissistic drunk.

At some point, I must have fallen asleep on the staircase because I was woken up when Billy tripped over me and fell down the stairs. Oh boy, did I cop it that night!

After all, what the fuck was I doing on the stairs listening in to adult conversations? To admit to being worried about what he might do to my mum would have meant sure death, so I stayed quiet. My silence did not stop him from beating me half to death that night. Clearly, he hadn't had enough fighting for one night. I was only about nine years old. Back then, the Cosby Show was a hit on TV and I used to dream that Bill Cosby was my dad because, in that show, he was such a cool dad. With the recent "guilty as charged" for child sexual abuse in Cosby's case, I guess I was better off with Billy. Perhaps the lesser of two evils.

Naturally, I continued to stay awake when they fought for many, many years but luckily for me I never got caught again.

My mum worked for a car hire company back in those days and had made friends with some fabulous Greek people who owned a yacht. We spent a fair bit of time with them. They were so normal and such a beautiful, loving family. I think they gave me hope to keep going. We used to visit them at their home in Cape Town (not my dad, he wasn't welcome) and I honest to God felt normal and happy whenever we were there.

I truly believe in the saying friends are either in your life for a season, a reason or a lifetime. This beautiful Greek family are still in my life forty years on. The friendship is extraordinary and the love I have for them is something very precious to me. So precious that when I got married for the second time a few years ago, I was walked down the aisle by one of them and his wife helped me get into my dress and made my cake and was there for me all day. We all spent five wonderful days together as they flew over especially. I see them every time I am in Melbourne because they are my family.

I don't think they actually realise that during some of the darkest days of my life, their love and friendship kept me going. My lifetime friends. Even though we weren't in close contact for many years, that friendship kept me alive. In some of the darkest times of my life, I would think about them often and know if I needed them, they would be there with the front door and arms wide open.

They made me realise the power of love and of being kind as well as the value of life.

12
Mum's had enough

So eventually the day arrives that my mum has finally grown a pair and decides to call it quits. But being married to Billy, you can't just up and say you want a divorce. No way, that would be like signing your own death warrant. If you haven't realised by now that it's Billy's way or the highway, you need to pay more attention. This had to be a very carefully planned exit. After all, no one leaves Billy. Billy does the leaving.

My mum tried to convince us that it would be easier if she left on her own initially. That meant we would have to stay behind with Billy. This naturally, scared the shit out of me. I was probably only about ten years old then and knowing how volatile he was, I knew this would not end well. But I was also proud of my mum for finally getting the courage to leave that I wasn't going to make it harder for her even though I was only a kid. Surely, she knew better as an adult?

Or maybe not.

It's a Saturday afternoon. Family fun time. Just kidding, another shit-filled weekend of screaming and shouting and fighting. Situation normal. Except Billy doesn't know what's about to happen and we are quietly shitting ourselves that everything goes to plan and Mum gets out. In one piece. And alive.

The plan is for her to exit the back door and run around the house to the road when the bailiff knocks on the front door to deliver the divorce papers. Yes, that's the way it was done back then. No instant, easy-peasy divorce-sign-here-and you're-free divorce. Oh no, the bailiff has to deliver the court orders. Surely this poor bastard couldn't like his job? Believe me, if he liked it before Billy, I can guarantee he didn't like it after Billy.

So Billy goes to see who's at the door and Mum does a runner as planned. The next thirty minutes were almost surreal. Billy tells the bailiff to wait a moment "while I fetch my glasses". Silly, silly bailiff to fall for that one. We are delivering divorce (read, you loser) papers to a man who doesn't like to lose. Bailiff waits patiently until Billy returns. With a nine-iron golf club. Oh my, the shit's about to hit the fan.

Forty years on, I can sometimes giggle about those thirty minutes. But not much really. Billy was not a large man but what he lacked in height, he sure made up with his vicious temper. The bailiff started running for his life and he made it to his car with Billy hot on his heels. Before he could start the car, Billy laid into it with his nine iron, completely destroying it. Windscreen and windows shattered, metal buckled. I think the bailiff was in too much shock to simply start the fucking engine and hightail it out of there.

Next on Billy's shit list was my mother and her lawyer who were about three hundred metres from our front gate on the other side of the road. What complete stupidity made them stay, I have no idea. I thought my mother would be long gone by then. I remember Billy running towards them with his golf club with murder in his eyes and heart. The lawyer copped a blow to his body with the said golf club and my mum took off, thank God. The lawyer's car was destroyed within seconds and thankfully, for him and my mum, the cops showed up about that time. Billy was still screaming abuse when he was escorted back into our yard. My sister and I were looking out the second-floor window, completely wild-eyed and in shock.

And then everyone else left. To this day, it amazes me that the cops only broke up a bad situation but did not stay to check if there was anyone else in the house that might be in danger nor even encourage anyone to press charges. Back then, it was a domestic situation and the police had little power to get involved. They simply cleared the situation off the street and out of the public eye.

My childhood well and truly ended right there. Billy decided I was Mum's accomplice in all of this and I knew about what was going to happen and I didn't tell him. I was a traitor. How my sister wasn't a traitor too, I'll never know. What I do know is I copped the full extent of Billy's rage.

Billy was so angry, he was almost incoherent. I copped an earful of rage, how bad I was, that I wasn't his child, that I was a traitor and on and on it went. I also copped a few blows from the almost-destroyed nine iron. Turns out this was all my fault. Go figure. The rage continued for days.

Next on the list of my punishment was to destroy my new Steinway piano. Because. She. That. Mad. Bitch. Mother. Of. Mine had bought it for me only weeks before. He knew how much I loved that piano and who knows, if my life had been a little more normal, I might have been a pianist today. I was happiest when I was playing my Steinway. Note to self: never admit to loving anything too much with Billy

57

as your father. The next tool of destruction was the electric saw. By the time he reduced my piano to a pile of rubble, I almost wished he would use that chainsaw to lop my head off. But no, Billy was not that kind.

I was then locked in my room to think about what a terrible person I was. For two weeks, no food, no water, nothing. If it hadn't been for my sister sneaking saucers of water or milk and the odd slice of bread under the door when Billy was passed out, I probably wouldn't be writing this book.

Day three of being imprisoned, there was more fun to be had. Unfortunately, Billy knew how much I loved my three guinea pigs. Back then, he had a "security" business which basically meant we had three extremely vicious Doberman dogs permanently chained up in different corners of our yard during the day. At night, the dogs were taken out to industrial areas accompanied by a black guard, to patrol warehouses to ensure there were no break-ins. Only Billy and the guards could handle these dogs. We were always warned to steer clear of them and I can assure you, on the odd times I went too close to them by accident, I regretted it. They would have killed me without hesitation. This, added to the environment of our home, I guess. It was almost as dangerous inside as it was outside. Dad got you inside, dogs got you outside. Charming childhood memories.

Billy was drunk and in a state of great excitement when he yelled up to my first-floor window. He told me to open the window and watch. He told me if I looked away, he would come to get me from my room and feed me to the dogs. So I watched. I watched him let my guinea pigs out of their cages and I watched them running away and being caught and being torn from limb to limb by the guard dogs. Their screaming still rings in my ears today. My dad's insane laughter during this act of extreme cruelty still rings in my ears to this day. He laughed so much, the tears rolled down his face and he had to hold his tummy. It was sore from laughing. It was sore from laughing at the look of terror on my face and my hysterical screaming and crying at the fate of my pets. At that point, I realised how mad he truly was. Surely it is not normal to enjoy killing your child's pet whilst making said child watch?

The next couple of years went by in a blur. The divorce was ugly. My sister and I had to testify in court so many times we lost count. Was our dad violent? Did he hit our mother? Did they fight a lot? Were we scared of him? Honest to God, adults are sometimes totally clueless.

Billy made sure he packed up the Empangeni house and put all our furniture into storage. He was going to make sure that my mum never saw any of that furniture again. When it came to dividing up the matrimonial assets, he acted like he didn't have a clue what had become of the furniture. There was nothing my mum could do really. The courts were a bit of a joke, I think.

We were living with my mum again and Billy got us every second weekend. During the week we got the vitriol from my mum about how we had to say this and say that to ensure my dad never saw us again. She continually reinforced what an arsehole he was and that is pretty much all we heard out of her mouth for years. Of course, she was right, but by that time I was so traumatised and I also disliked her a little for leaving us behind. Welcome to our new world where your parents pit you against each other in the bloody fight for custody.

And every second weekend, we got the nicest dad you can possibly imagine. Billy was truly sorry (truly sorry my arse) for all he had done and said and wanted to make it up to us. He was amazing and we were little. And we wanted our dad to be normal and love us, so we didn't realise how he was manipulating the situation to his advantage. He was a cunning prick. How on earth could we go back to court and say bad things about him when he was the best dad on earth? The sins of the fathers.

My mum remained bitter for years and years and my dad remained a master manipulator. There were years of court cases where my sister and I had to testify against my mum or against my dad. Everything, and I mean everything, was used as evidence against one or the other parent. Old birthday cards were submitted, school reports, letters, everything and anything that could hurt the case of a parent against the other one.

In those days, children had to testify in court. Can you believe we were called to the stand? We had to say who we wanted to live with and why. Can you imagine doing that with both parents staring at you in a full courthouse? We had to answer the most invasive questions of life at home during our younger formative years. All the ugliness shared in public. I remain deeply surprised we weren't taken into foster care. Even today, I wonder how much a child has to suffer to be believed and rescued.

Anyway, they eventually divorced, and life went on. Life was even reasonably peaceful and happy for a change. We had changed schools. Again. And we lived with my mum and saw Billy every second weekend.

He always had a new woman or wife on these visits. If the relationship was reasonably new, as kids we knew that was a very good time to ask dad for a loan or extra pocket money. If he could show off in front of said new woman by peeling off and counting money and giving it to his "adorable children", it was a bonus for all of us. We got extra funds; Billy got adoration (and probably a good blowjob); the new lady thought she'd met a man with a big heart so everyone was happy.

Not for long though. There was simply no peace when Billy was around. Life was like a roller coaster ride. And about to get a little bumpy.

13
Knocking on Heaven's (or Hell's) Door

Just when you think you deserve how peaceful life is and even start to enjoy it, Billy finds a way to rock the boat.

By this time, Billy and my mum seemed to be able to be civil to each other so pick-ups and drop-offs weren't as stressful. He arrived one Friday afternoon with flowers for my mother and lollies for us. To this day, I believe he never got over my mum or more to the point, never got over being dumped by her and he never stopped trying to get her back. I don't think it was because his heart was broken; more likely, his ego was bruised. He didn't like to lose.

So it's Billy's weekend and he arrives to collect us. He asks for a few moments alone with my mother. We were never too comfortable with this because we always thought he might do her in, but we did what we were told and went to our rooms. When we were called back to the lounge, we walked into floods of tears on both sides.

Billy had been diagnosed with cancer. Terminal cancer. So terminal, he only had about three months to live. The lying bastard. He begged my mother to allow him to move back in so we could be "a proper family" again for whatever time he had left. A proper family again? When the fuck had we ever been a proper family?

Naturally, we were all very sad and felt that would be the right thing to do. Let Billy back for his last few months. Thankfully my mother was a lot smarter than that and started asking awkward questions about who was his oncologist, etc.? Awkward questions if you're lying for sure. Billy was a little vague with his answers and said he didn't want my mum to accompany him to the oncologist because he wanted to protect her from how bad things actually were. We should've known right there and then that he was feeding us a line of shit because he hadn't protected us from anything bad in our lives, so why start now?

It didn't take too long for the truth to surface and Billy was exposed as the manipulative, lying little prick he was. Goes without saying, he laughed his head off and said it was worth a try and then left. Not the first, nor the last time in my life that I would be exposed to his cunning. I have never quite gotten over the fact that he actually enjoyed his cunning, manipulative behaviour. He thought he was quite hilarious actually and if he had a conscience, it was very well hidden. He really didn't care who he hurt. As long as he got his own way. He remains one of the mysteries of my world, even though he carked it years ago.

This father of mine, who completely believed in himself and did whatever he liked, when he liked. No matter who he hurt along the way. This sadistic man, who could charm the birds from the trees. When Billy was in charming mode, he was the nicest guy under the sun and many, many people got sucked in by that side of Billy. And many people regretted it.

14
Time for a little trip

I think I was about twelve when Billy picked us up for a weekend away. The weekend away turned into fifteen months away. He was a little upset that his terminal cancer scare hadn't worked on my mother so came up with another way to annoy her and get her to consider reuniting our happy little family.

He sure didn't give up easily. After all, this was a few years after the divorce and he was still trying to get her back. Don't get me wrong, he is not heartbroken. He simply does not like to lose. Or maybe I am being a little harsh and this was really true love? When he was not knocking on our door with a sob story to get his family back, he was still partying like there's no tomorrow. He is still drinking himself stupid and screwing everything that moves. But Billy has many different personalities and in front of us, he is the poor sad, heartbroken man who simply wants his family back together again.

I'm going to cut this chapter short because there is still so much to write. Billy basically kidnapped us and took us across the border into the Transkei. This ensured my mother couldn't fight for us from the other side of the border as South Africa had no jurisdiction there.

The crafty little prick actually stole our passports on that

Friday afternoon when he said he needed to go to the toilet and off we went. My mum, my sister and I were a little unit by then and we hated leaving her alone to go with him for the weekend, but we had no choice. The court had spoken and if she didn't abide by the court orders, there would be legal trouble, i.e., she could go to jail.

We arrived in the shit hole of a town of Umtata a couple of days later and moved into a caravan which became home for the next fifteen months. Why did we always end up in shitholes for towns with this mad parent? My sister was sent to boarding school, God knows why, and I drew the jackpot of having to keep house for him while he worked, played and drank. I did go to school every day but had strict instructions to return every day by a certain time, to clean and cook his evening curry. God help me if he called and I wasn't home. Clearly, not a great time for making friends and I was at such a vulnerable age. Anyway, I went to school every day and became his slave the rest of the time. Happy days.

Meanwhile, Billy would make his daily calls to my mum telling her if she wanted to see her kids again (alive), she would have to agree to remarry him. A fate worse than death, surely. At the time we were devastated that she wouldn't agree. We hated living with him and we just wanted to go home to Mum but my God, she stood her ground. In hindsight, I'm glad she did but I can tell you those fifteen months were a complete nightmare. Master manipulator Billy would wind me up every day before that call so that I was in tears when he made me speak to my mother. I suppose me crying my eyes out and begging to come home was part of his master plan. My mum cried and I cried. Billy either got into a rage or if he'd had enough whiskey, he would simply sit there grinning, somehow believing that his plan was going to work out. Sadist much?

At the fourteen-and-a-half-month mark, Billy got tired of having the responsibility of children. Not sure how he got tired of having that responsibility because he didn't actually have that responsibility. We weren't treated like his kids. We were just his slaves. We were the pawns he was using to get his own way. His life was a blur of drinking, parties, womanising and generally doing what he liked. He didn't behave like a father. He never even helped me with my homework. He didn't cook. Didn't clean. Didn't provide me with fatherly advice so I am baffled at how he grew tired of the "responsibility" of having children. Beats the fuck out of me. Surely you have to *be* a father for a while before you get tired of being one? His lordship felt it was time to return us to our mother.

So we loaded up the ancient VW station wagon. And. Headed. To. The. Local. Pub. I shit you not. My sister and I sat in the car for several hours waiting for him to finish drinking. He finally got into the car, drunk as the proverbial skunk, screamed at me to drive the fucking car to my bitch of a mother's house. And passed out. I was barely thirteen years old and didn't have a driver's license. In fact, I could barely see over the steering wheel and had had limited driving lessons. But we were going home to Mum, so drive I did.

Billy woke up a few times during the 1300-kilometre trip, mainly to tell me to pull into the next pub where he would spend as many hours as he liked filling up his tank and playing pool with the locals. We sat in the car like we were told to do and at odd intervals he would fling in a packet or two of chips and a pie and a drink, gaily telling us he was on his last drink and would be right out. They must've been large drinks back then because two or three hours later, he would lurch to the car and pass out after telling me to hit the road.

My sister and I somehow enjoyed the trip. We talked over the snoring and farting and told each other jokes to stay awake.

Two days later we pulled into the driveway of my mum's house. I think I was so excited, I accidentally banged the passenger door into the post-box and there was hell to pay for that. Fuck you, Billy, I was thirteen years old and had just driven 1300 kilometres without an incident, so yeah, just fuck you.

We were overjoyed to be home. Bill slunk away in his dented station wagon, hurling insults at all of us. He had just wasted fifteen more months of all our lives because my mum was not giving in to his tricks. Not now, not ever. Once bitten, she had no intention of ever becoming his wife again. There is a God, then. Because we had no real interest in becoming that happy family again either.

Life went on. We went back to our old schools. Billy went looking for his next victim. Sorry, wife.

15
Wife # 2

Billy had lost interest in pursuing his happy little family so we were, in a sense, free to live our lives for a few years. He was always up to some trick or another, but we were teenagers then, damaged as all fuck, but simply trying to be teenagers and do what teenagers do.

Life was pretty sweet. Boyfriends. Friends. The giving up of the gold v-chip. Love and sex. Sex and love. Drinking. Partying. Just the normal life of a teenager. Mum was partying like it was 1969. Out every night with a new man and generally making up for all her "lost" years with Billy. She was having the time of her life and we were too, in a sense. We had very little guidance or supervision. We had massive chips on our shoulders and fear in our hearts but we were "free" to be as normal as we could be.

Free from the maniacal behaviour of our father that is. There were no boundaries. We had no clue how to behave or what was acceptable and what was taboo. We had been raised in fear and were just grateful to be alive, but we had no clue how to live. Conditioning is a terrible thing. If my mum or my boyfriend wasn't screaming at me or abusing me in some way, I would make sure I behaved in such a way as to get their attention. I didn't know how to respond to kindness and I certainly did not understand what was required to have a good, solid relationship or marriage. I still don't to some degree.

I was very damaged and bruised by life to date so I was a real target for anyone kind or nice to me. I had no idea how to behave in a relationship. Some would argue I still have no idea ☺.

Those years flew by in a blur, as they do for most of us. I had contact with Billy during those years and I watched while he destroyed another woman, another marriage.

Estie was a really lovely lady. Rich beyond imagination but you'd never pick it up. Of course, Billy picked it and I think the money was what he was after. The fact that the money came with a not unattractive wife didn't faze him. I may have mentioned what a calculating bastard he was. She stood no chance against the force of his charm. He literally swept her off her feet. We did not meet her until they were married which was probably part of Billy's cunning. He knew he couldn't risk losing this goldmine by introducing his damaged little angels too early in the piece.

I really liked Estie, but then I liked most of his wives. He had good taste in women. I never understood why she married him but I never voiced my opinions. Billy would have killed me for sure. I figured she was smart enough and she would eventually know she had made a terrible mistake. Turns out it didn't take that long anyway.

He kept the façade of a happy, normal husband going for a few months anyway. She thought she'd hit the jackpot. He *knew* he'd hit the jackpot! I watched with some interest because I knew the shit would hit the fan at some point. Once Billy got what he wanted, he became bored quickly. Plus, he had a shitload of newly-acquired cash to spend, so the mask came away pretty quickly.

It didn't take him long to wheedle his way into her company after he'd wheedled his way into her pants, that is. She had a company she had established with her late husband which she continued to run after he popped his clogs. It was a manufacturing company in Johannesburg that printed money. Billy very quickly became the Chief Financial Officer (fuck that is so funny on so many levels. My dad the pseudo-accountant) complete with a seat on the board. Billy had control and was suddenly a respected businessman with all the power and prestige that came with it.

I'm sure all his former employers were quietly cursing and of course, Billy was giving them all the middle finger. He was in his element.

Given his new position in the business world, he had to have all the fringe benefits that came with it. Palatial houses were purchased, Mercedes-Benzes, boats and memberships to all kinds of exclusive clubs. Billy was the man about town.

Estie was blissfully cock-struck still disbelieving of her luck. How could she have met this wonderful man? She had adored her first husband and had an amazing marriage and so she was firmly under the impression she had hit the love jackpot again. She was so lucky!

Until she wasn't of course. Once Billy had everything he'd ever wanted, money *and most importantly*, he was up there with the rich and richer, he would become very quickly, well, *bored*. He had the *respect* of many because of his position in the business world, more money than he could spend, a beautiful wife, amazing houses and all the bells and whistles that money bought, but he was bored.

You see Billy was a renegade at heart and if he wasn't

stirring things up and causing havoc wherever he went, he got bored. He had to be constantly challenged and the challenge of bagging the bride and the seat at the board had already worn off.

He was like a child really. And he became my child from thereon.

Estie slowly became aware that she had married a dud. By then the company was in the red and she was facing professional and personal bankruptcy. Billy had resigned as CFO long before. He knew he had depleted the corporate bank accounts and he was way too smart to still be involved once the investigators arrived to find out where the money had gone.

He had also shown his wife what a complete knob he was by this stage. She was no longer in awe of him and certainly no longer thought she had found love again. He was mean and abusive; he drank like a fish and he cared about her about as much as he cared about anything else in life: not much. Let. Me. Be. Clear. Leopards. Do. Not. Change. Their. Spots.

The fatalities in this marriage went beyond Estie. She had a daughter from her first marriage whom Billy (during the charming stage), had insisted on adopting. Thanks, Billy, I have a half-sister out there who has the same name as I used to have. I don't see her any more and Estie died of a heart attack (and probably a broken heart and soul) a few years after she left Billy, at age fifty-two.

When Estie realised the extent of what she had done by marrying the maniac, we had long conversations and became quite close. She eventually confided in me that she was bankrupt and all she really had was the furniture in the house they lived in. This furniture had mostly belonged to her and her ex-husband and she didn't want to lose it all. So I eventually told her that if she wanted to keep the furniture, we would have to plan a midnight evacuation and I would help her. After all, I had seen first-hand how spiteful Billy could be and my mum's furniture was never found after he "sent it to storage".

The houses were in Billy's name but that would not be for long. The bank and the fraud commission weren't far away and all his wealth would be reclaimed before long.

Billy went away on a business trip (read: Billy went away to get hammered and screw women that were not his wife) and Estie and I sprang into action. I was about nineteen at this stage. The two of us packed and loaded the truck all night long. Estie packed everything that she wanted and by dawn, we pulled out of the driveway.

Billy returned that afternoon to an empty house and no wife and child. Naturally, he called me (his mother) and in an absolute rage screamed at me about what a total fucking bitch Estie was and that "she'd cleaned me out". Of course, he insinuated that I had helped her but I stayed schtum. I still laugh at the irony of the statement as to who actually cleaned whom out?! But in true form, Billy never admitted guilt, never had a conscience and never really ever saw the wickedness of his ways. He was untouchable and beyond reproach in his own mind.

Sadly, I never saw Estie again.

Like many of the next wives, they decided that they wanted nothing further to do with Billy and therefore nothing to do with me. They literally went into hiding and disappeared.

I liked most of Billy's wives and was close to a few of them. The fact that I was tarred with the same brush as he still annoys me. I can't really blame them though as he really did do his utmost to destroy their lives, simply by being who he was. Simply by being the complete lunatic he was, a man with multiple personalities and so many hang-ups, you simply never knew which Billy was which.

But he was my dad and life went on.

My first loyalty was supposed to be with him, wasn't it?

16
On the run again

Billy felt absolute rocks that his wife had left him. He was more annoyed at the fact she had outsmarted him and run off with the furniture. He was the boss of the world after all. Only he called the shots. For Estie to "do this to him after all he had done for her" was unacceptable.

He could do fuck-all about it though as Estie's rage had escalated by then and the Fraud Squad were intent on locking up his skinny arse for a long time to come. Yep, Estie had told them everything she knew with a little help from me and they were onto him.

He ducked and dived in true Billy style for a year or two and I had no contact with him for a while.

The next time I heard from him was in the form of a desperate call for help from Hong Kong. The long and the short of it was that he had proposed to Jenny and Jenny had said yes. Stupid woman. They were blissfully engaged for five seconds and then Jenny called it off. Clever lady. Billy could not deal with this and had flown into a rage. An argument had naturally ensued and then in his typical pig-headed-no one-dumps-me mode, he had kicked her out of their hotel room.

He then proceeded to drink Hong Kong dry. Drown his sorrows, so to speak. When he resurfaced a few days later, he called me. These were some of the things he was ranting. "LuLu, I can't go on. I am going to jump from the 34th floor of my hotel." *Happy jumping Dad.* "Why do these women continue to hurt me? How is your mother, the mole? I can't go on LuLu. Please come and help me." *Just jump dad, off you go. It's not that far down. Go on. Jump. Please. Just fucking do it.*

Of course, I have to save him. He. Is. My. Dad. He needs me. So I get on the next flight to Hong Kong feeling dreadfully ill. After all that the man had put me through, I couldn't bear the thought of him topping himself and not being around any more. Seriously peeps, the sins of the father, eh? Clearly, I was more damaged than even I knew because I really didn't want him to die. Also, strangely enough, I had always been the child that kept the peace in the family. My role was always the glue, keeping everyone happy and together. It's not that easy to change who you were conditioned to be, so of course, I flew to Hong Kong. I had to make sure Billy was okay. That conditioning is still with me today. Sadly. I always strive for peace and sometimes I give people way too many chances, way more than they deserve. In the name of peace. Because that is conditioning people. Gotta fix things. Gotta fix people. Sad but true.

I arrived in Hong Kong in the early evening and the concierge rings and rings Billy's room but there is no answer. I figure he jumped. I eventually persuade the guy that my dad could be dead so he has to take me up to his room, pronto. We go up in the lift to the 34th floor and all the way up, I am totally convinced Billy is dead. Silly. Fucking. Me.

We arrive in his room and he is merrily making his way through a bottle of scotch. He sees me and the biggest smile breaks out on his face. "Lulu, you came. I can't believe you're here. Do you wanna scotch?"

Concierge departs quietly thinking I'm a total fuckwit. I can't really blame him, can I?

I lay into Billy. "WTF Billy? What the actual Fuck Billy? You're supposed to be depressed and about to end your life? You're supposed to be suicidal?"

In true Billy style, he roars with laughter and says that's in the past and now that I'm with him, we can go have a drink together and enjoy Hong Kong. Fuck Jenny. Who is this Jenny you refer to anyway? What a cluster. Why could I not have. A. Normal. Fucking. Father?

He. Is. Such. An. Annoying. Little. Prick.

We hit Hong Kong together. I try to tell him he has to think about his actions. He has to change his life somehow. He simply cannot go on as before. Surely you realise you cannot keep hurting and misleading people like this, Billy? And Billy, naturally, says fuck them all. If they can't handle Billy in their boring lives, they can just rearrange the following words in an everyday, acceptable fashion. Off. Fuck. Billy's way or the highway.

One frustrating, expensive trip to Hong Kong later, I return to South Africa and my life. I have a business to run after all.

Billy disappears again for a year or so.

17
Keep on running

Love that song, but it has no relevance to this chapter. Billy resumes his life in Johannesburg as if Jenny never happened and as if I never flew to Hong Kong for him to cry on my shoulder. On my credit card. No reimbursement here, people, just doing my job as the daughter of one selfish little prick.

I think about this trip often. I think about when I was a teenager and used to ask him for some extra pocket money and his answer was always, "I don't have any money. All I've got is the skin on my balls." Well, Dad, the skin on your balls is not acceptable currency out there in the real world. And his response, "Well that's all I've got, kid."

But my God, if there was a vagina involved, Billy somehow found the money. Shits me to this day how the money appeared if there was a chance of Billy getting laid or starting a new love affair.

Due to Billy's many "deals" and just-under-the-radar criminal activities plus his day job, he lived quite a luxurious lifestyle. He had an enormous house in one of the better suburbs in Johannesburg and entertained as if the world would never end. Parties at Billy's house were revered. His so-called friends all loved an invitation to Billy's. A never-ending supply of scotch, Champagne, some really smart people and there was always an overabundance of single hot women. Who knows where they came from? In hindsight, I think I know what and who these women were... after all, you never saw them twice.

Anyway, the parties at Billy's pad were always legendary and I was at his house a lot. Dad was the epitome of the great entertainer and host and everyone had a marvellous time. I used to take some of my friends around (the hardier ones) and it was always fabulous. Lazing around the pool, swimming, bar fully stocked and food to die for. Billy was always a showman and he did the best fish on the barbie I have ever known. I think it was what he learnt growing up in Kenya. The most divine whole fish, filled with herbs, spices and chillies, grilled whole on the barbecue wrapped in kilometres of foil. I can taste it as I type.

Don't be fooled though, because I wasn't. I remember arriving at his house early on a Sunday morning. He was up early too and was loading a skip bin. Full of family photos and even more painful, photos of my sister and me at various stages of us growing up. That's right, just throwing away all those memories. I'm pleased to say I treasure all my children's photos, perhaps more so. I guess considering my dad threw all of ours in the skip bin, there was another lesson in there somewhere. It was pretty clear that Billy lived for Billy. Damaged as all fuck but it is what it is. As his children, we really had no value to him. We were simply a liability from birth.

Billy had many different women on his arm at these gatherings, almost a different one every week. Really lovely women, I'll never understand the attraction. Actually, I do understand the attraction. I am, after all, his daughter and have made some disastrous choices in men who are or were just like him. Sins of the fathers.

It didn't take long for things to change. Again. The proverbial hit the fan and the funds dried up. He lost his job, God knows why, and then lost the enormous house. I guess the women and the friends dried up then too. People tend to disperse when the money and the fun times run out the door.

Billy went underground for a while and then resurfaced in the form of a poor white man. He had nothing and no one to look after him so he showed up on my doorstep. Not just showing up as a normal out-of-work person but as a fully bloodied down-on-my-luck type person.

After I'd fed him a scotch and removed the glass shards from his head, I managed to somehow get to the truth. He'd been involved in a hit and run. He'd run. He thinks the other driver was killed. Charming. And you *ran away from the scene Billy?* You might have tried to save the other driver. Maybe. If you were a normal person. Oh boy, here we go again. We put him in the spare room once he'd had enough scotch and tried to figure out what to do. Billy was in a bad way.

In true Billy style, a good belly full of food and scotch and a good sleep later, he woke up full of balls. He was going to face the day. Unfortunately, I had to face it with him. We went to the police station where Billy explained (with tears in his eyes), that he was scared the night before and that made him take off. He wanted to do whatever he had to, to make things right. Please hand my father his fucking Oscar award, for the best acting of the decade.

Long story short, he was relieved of all charges and life went on. The other driver survived with multiple life-long injuries, but Billy was off the hook. Yet again. I swear to God, this man had the devil on his shoulder because who could possibly survive and thrive in this environment, I ask myself.

Only one person. Billy. More fucking lives than the proverbial cat.

He lived with me and my fiancé for three months, causing trouble left, right, and you guessed it, centre. Stuck his nose into everything. He criticised everything. My fiancé was a lot older than me. Laugh my arse off at this one. Daddy issues anyone? Anyway, Billy was horrified I was marrying someone who was almost his age. Looking back, I guess I was looking for a father figure. Hell, some form of right and wrong, some form of guidance, would have been nice. As an aside, that first marriage of mine ended up lasting over a decade. A miracle in itself really, and I have two beautiful children from it. I am still friends with my first husband to this day but let's be clear, I had no idea how to be a wife, let alone a mother. Anyway, this book isn't about me so let's keep going.

Billy caused havoc in my world again for those three months. Once he settled in and thought he ruled my roost again, his behaviour was truly despicable. Criticising me, criticising my soon-to-be-husband, criticising the food I cooked and the whiskey I bought. Nasty, nasty Daddy.

Let's just say I allowed him to stay long enough to walk me down the aisle and then we cut him free. The wedding was reasonably peaceful. Billy's speech was woeful. He truly was all about Billy. He drank too much, annoyed me, annoyed my mother and thankfully, left early.

Billy went under the radar for another six months.

18
Shit in the shop. Again.

On and off over the next couple of years, I see Billy in Johannesburg pubs. God only knows how he was making his living, but he was hanging in there and staying out of trouble, to the best of my knowledge.

Shows how much I knew, because the next thing I know, I'm getting a phone call from Perth in Western Australia. From. Billy. "Darling Lu, I am sooo happy and I'm getting married!"

Whoop-de-fucking-doo Billy!

"LuLu, can you please come to my wedding?"

My response was, "No Dad, I can't. I have a business to run and I can't make this wedding. But I promise I'll come to the next one!"

Boom. Clearly not the right thing to say. Billy told me to go fuck myself and I didn't hear from him for another year at least. I thought it was quite funny, but then who am I? Billy's way or the highway.

I did go home to Perth later that year but I was not allowed access to his new bride. Billy and I met in a pub instead. He said he didn't trust me to keep quiet with his new wife. Keep quiet about what Billy? Keep quiet about my real life, LuLu, no one would marry him after all, if they knew his life real story. Sad, but true. At least he admitted it. Only that once did he admit it.

I did feel sorry for him though because clearly, he didn't like himself very much. This was why he had to continually recreate himself. Even he didn't like who he was. I was, of course, an adult by now and tried my best to understand the mess that was Billy. I never did. Talk about issues, my God. His and mine.

Anyway, the marriage lasted less than a year. Pretty bloody predictable.

I hate to say it but it was good for a long time with him living a million miles away in Australia. I guess I got a chance to focus on my own life for a while. I had a business to run, a baby on the way and no time for drama.

The political situation and general unrest in South Africa were cause for concern, especially with a new baby. I carried a Smith & Wesson 38 special revolver in a holster on my body at all times back then. And I knew how to use it. In Johannesburg at that time, I would go for shooting lessons every second Saturday and then lunch with my friends. Crime was at an all-time high. Car hijacking was extremely common and a lot of people lost their cars and some, their lives. The hijackers felt rocks. It wasn't just about stealing your car. Apartheid had instilled them with hatred for white (rich) people and they really enjoyed tormenting and torturing you whilst stealing your car. And if you were lucky, they let you live.

Rape was also at an all-time high. White women raped by black men mostly. It was really scary. I bought the gun after I saw a billboard with a gorgeous blonde woman holding a gun with the slogan: "You can't rape a 38 special". We had Billy's 347 Magnum in the safe at home too, but we never used it. Billy had this gun because John Wayne and Clint Eastwood used to use this type of gun in the movies. Laughing out loud right now. Ol' Billy. He obsessed about being John Wayne or Clint Eastwood.

I remember driving my near new luxury German car home one afternoon when I was held up at a set of traffic lights close to home. Thankfully it was before my daughter was born. I was quite ballsy back then. I wonder who instilled that in me. Anyway, long story short, I got to hang on to my car and my life but I ended up shooting one of the hijacker's legs off. You messed with the wrong woman lol. Don't mess with Billy's daughter.

I could protect myself but I was terrified that something would happen to our little girl so we made the decision to leave South Africa and head back to Australia. I was going home and my husband and child cashed in on my Aussie passport for visas and we were gone.

I think about heading out of the frying pan into the fire here. It's not quite that bad but we were leaving a dangerous country but heading towards Billy. Perhaps we should have stayed in Africa. Lesser of two evils.

19
Billy does Australia again

We settled in Perth where I was born. Billy was on the edges of our lives back then. He didn't need me, because he was ducking and diving again, and mostly he worked away. "Away" meaning he worked in shithole towns many hundreds of kilometres from Perth and only came back when he felt like it or to visit his parents.

He had no real interest in meeting my children, his grandchildren. No real interest in me for the first couple of years in Perth. He'd call now and again or I'd run into him at his parents' house but that was really it. It was very peaceful. From a Billy perspective anyway. I was going through my own marital issues at the time so it was probably a blessing to be able to deal with those in isolation and not with him as well. Certainly did not consider asking either of my parents for marital advice, that's for sure!

I do remember hearing about a couple more marriages during these years but I didn't crack an invite to them. Nor did most of his family. By this time, Billy would be in his early sixties and I guess he was slowing down a bit.

He went underground for many years at this time, resurfacing on and off over the years. He didn't need me, and I certainly did not need his dramas. I had never really known a real father, so I knew how to live without one. Situation normal. I would see him at family events like Christmas or funerals. I remember meeting wife number six at his mother's funeral. Billy adored his mother as did I, so it was a very sombre occasion. I don't remember speaking much with his new bride.

A few months later I received a call from Billy saying we should catch up. As usual, we met at some bar. I asked him how married life was going and he said she left. I think this one lasted about a year. What a cow! Not. Seriously no one could put up with all his bullshit for too long. Such a sad, broken little man.

Years later when I was organising Billy's funeral, I had to produce a list of marriages and divorces, amongst other things. Still don't understand why. What the fuck has seven marriage certificates and seven divorce certificates got to do with sending someone on their final journey? Anyway, rules are rules. He kept most of his personal records in his black, locked briefcase so after breaking the code on that, I found most of what I needed. Thankfully the funeral director didn't insist on having sight of all the marriage and divorce certificates because otherwise, we would never have cremated the little bastard. I had to just tell him "to the best of my knowledge" and show him what I could find. During Billy's last few years, we had grown apart a lot so I didn't know every detail of his life, that's for sure.

Back to the bar. Billy produced some pretty convincing crocodile tears whilst telling me how much he missed me and wanted to be a bigger part of my life again. Yeah right. My first thought was what does the little fucker want but as I said before, he was a charming man and he honestly should have been on the stage. Man, could this man act. In a different life, he should have been an actor. He sure had the looks for it and, I have no doubt, he would have walked away with many Oscars.

Being the complete fucktard that I am, I kind of softened at his words. Maybe this little girl (who was knocking on the door of her fortieth year) was finally going to get a real dad. Gullible. Idiot. That. You. Are. Seriously? Ah well, what was there to lose right? All he wanted was to meet my children and have a real relationship with us before he donned his oak cloak. I just felt sorry for this old man who seemed to have lost his vitality and spark. And imagination.

A few home visits ensued. He would drop around now and again pretending to be a real father and grandfather. I didn't trust him to hang around so just took things at face value. Besides I had a busy, full life so didn't focus all of my attention on Billy. This irked him I know. He always had to be the centre of everyone's world.

One day he dropped by and said he had been through a few hard times. I assume the last divorce settlement had taken a fair share of his dwindling bank account. Seven divorces must have cost him a bit but then I'm sure he made up for it by marrying a couple of cash cows in between. Problem with Billy was that he made and lost many fortunes over his lifetime.

He started asking to borrow money. I was rather tempted to tell him all I had was the skin on my balls but didn't have the heart to. Bottom line was I didn't have any extra cash anyway. He was persistent. So was I.

I had to question how skint he could be considering he rocked up in Mercedes Benz 4-wheel drive every time. When I questioned him, he said it was the only thing he owned outright and his only form of transport. I said he may have to sell it then and use public transport. I thought he would blow a valve he was so upset at the mere thought of public transport. Amazing how a person such as Billy still had absolute delusions of grandeur. He was totally horrified at the thought of having to board a bus or a train!

He was very much feeling sorry for himself as he hadn't been able to find work for a while at this point. I did feel for him but I had two small children to raise so I was not going to be parting with any dollars. Besides he never, ever paid it back to me so I was not taking any chances.

One day he showed up and said he had come up with a really good idea. I was immediately suspicious because the only person who usually benefitted from his grandiose plans was Billy. He suggested I buy the Mercedes. He said it would be great for carting the kids around. I already owned a Mercedes sedan and felt no urge to buy a 4-wheel drive version, but he literally pleaded and begged and told me I'd be helping him out enormously.

I caved in eventually. He said if I gave him $2000, it was mine. This would help him out and I'd have a fully paid-up second car. I am such a suck. The deal was done. I am such a suck.

Two weeks later the debt collectors knocked on my door and told me if I couldn't come up with the arrear's payments, they were taking the car. Turns out Billy owed $12,000 on the vehicle. I gave them the keys.

I then drove to his mother's house to kill him. I knew he was staying there because he was down and out and unemployed.

My grandmother told me she hadn't seen him since the weekend. He'd packed a suitcase the day he sold me the "fully paid for" car and was gone.

With my $2000. Clearly, it didn't matter if you were the guy's daughter and shared a blood bond. He really didn't care who he screwed over. I am such a suck.

Fuck you, Billy. The fucking wheel turns.

20
Running out of Options

A year or so later, I was waiting to board my flight in Sydney one afternoon to return home when I got a phone call from my uncle. He was distraught. I needed to get home as soon as possible because my dad is in trouble.

Too fucking bad, I said. If you see him, tell him I'd like my money back. My uncle explained to me that Billy was locked up in the detention centre at the airport and was about to be deported. Good. Let them deport the fucker.

I am such a gullible suck. Big tough words but I knew I would always try to "save him". Saving him was about as possible as containing the ash on a motorbike with an ashtray, but I always felt obligated to try.

They all knew I had some senior contacts in the police force and my dad needed my help. Lulu to the fucking rescue. Again.

21
London

So the very best I could do was get them to drop the charges and not deport him. Deporting the little prick meant he could never return to Australia, ever, and I just simply could not let that happen. Not even to him.

The authorities even gave him seventy-two hours to sort out his affairs and then board a flight to leave Australia for at least five years. Considering I did not trust the little fucker, that meant he had to move in with me so I could keep an eye on him.

I kid you not when I say he tried to do a runner at least twice in those seventy-two hours, even after I begged him not to. In this instance, my credibility was on the line because I'd got him out so I knew if he disappeared, I would be deeply embarrassed in my professional (and personal, because one always runs over into the other) capacity.

Those three days were rough. I didn't sleep. Who could, knowing the type of person he was? I had two young children at home, and I did not trust him around them at all. He was clearly down on his luck and drank more than normal, blaming the world for his problems. Same story, different day. It was never Billy's fault. The whole world was against him.

I asked him when he was going to tell me that he owed

so much on the car he had "sold" to me. He showed absolutely no remorse at robbing his own daughter. My dad. What a gentleman. What a gem. Jesus.

Finally, the three days were up, and we dropped him at the airport. I had to part with more cash because, of course, he had no means of setting himself up in London without a job and a place to live. I could have been loaded by now if I'd hung onto all the money instead of funding him. Selfish son-of-a-bitch he was. He even died with no will and no assets. I ended up putting myself in further debt after paying for a reasonable funeral and paying his debts. More on that later because he's not quite dead yet.

I breathe a little easier once the flight is in the air.

I hear from him from time to time, mainly with requests for money, which I dutifully send every time. Thousands and thousands and tens of thousands of dollars to keep the fucker alive, and with enough for alcohol and cigarettes. There is no end to my gullibility and kindness. I simply can't say no and even today, I will give people the benefit of the doubt, time after time. Again, and again and again. After all, I am conditioned that way. Sins of the fathers.

Like every other time in his life, Billy rises again. Gets a job, a nice flat and I don't hear from him much for a while. I even spend a weekend with him on a work trip to London.

And in true Billy form, it was one of the nicest weekends of my life. He talked a lot and seemed a lot more like a normal human being. We talked about my mum mostly, and his version of how their marriage was. It surprised me a lot to find out my mother was no angel, according to Billy.

It was a great weekend nonetheless and we spent a lot of time talking, watching the motorbike Grand Prix, and generally being closer than we had ever been in my life to date. Apparently, there was a good side to him. Such a pity it only came through once or twice in my life.

I still love watching the motorbike Grand Prix and always think about my dad during these times. Almost fondly.

He also finds wife #7 during this time. I didn't attend the wedding. I think he weddinged me out. I also didn't meet my sixth stepmother until years later. And Billy remains in London for his five years so there is a breather for me to focus on how to work out my own life, without blaming my childhood for all my many subsequent fuck-ups.

22
Stepmother #6

Oh, my fecking God. He has done it again. This lady is one of the nicest women I have ever met. A real lady. My question will never be answered. How the hell does he do it? All that handsomeness and charm at full voltage is simply irresistible and sadly, there are a lot of lonely women out there. I know all about that.

Back to Billy. Lotti is lovely, this wife of his. Wife number 7.

I receive a phone call one Saturday afternoon and it is Lotti. We speak for a while before she starts a strange type of interrogation of me. The first question that made me wonder what was going on was when she asked me how strange it was that I no longer speak with an American accent. I say what on earth are you talking about.

I'm pretty sure some of you may know what's coming next. LOL. Yep, Billy had turned into his former American self again when he met Lotti. A cool older American guy living in London. Lotti naturally thought she'd hit the jackpot. Interestingly, Lotti had only been married once, to a very good man and he had left her multiple businesses and factories to run when he passed. Billy naturally thought he'd hit the jackpot. Thank God I still can laugh because I'm howling now. It's Groundhog Day. Again.

Back to that phone call. She says I shouldn't be shy because she cannot wait to meet me after everything my dad has told her about his family. Fuck. What has he imagined up about us all in this new version of his life? It doesn't take long.

Lotti wants to know why my American accent is almost non-existent. Umm, perhaps because I'm not American? The story is *wild*. My life story is completely new to me and about as truthful and real as Snow White.

Okay, here we go. Lotti is gushing about what a wonderful man my father is. How she admires him for raising two little girls from the age of two years old and the other just a baby *when my mother died*. That's right, my mother died when I was a baby. Breast cancer apparently.

Funny because she was around my place for lunch today and I'm well into my forties. It gets worse. I have to give Billy points for creativity and imagination. Who thinks up this shit?

Lotti has so much respect for him, because he avoided women during the many lonely years he was raising us after my mother passed when I was a baby. He also nursed my mother through breast cancer for over a year and she died in his arms with his two little infants on the bed with her as the poor woman took her final breath. Fcuk. Me. Gently. What a man! So Lotti thinks she is his second wife because that's what he told her. Oh dear, what to do here. Talk about being in the middle of a shit sandwich.

This phone call is still going. Lotti wants to know if I'm still practising. Practising what, I ask? Practising trying to swallow this shit sandwich is about all I'm practising right now. No, that's not it. Turns out I am an esteemed lawyer who got my law degree in Phoenix. I was born there too. Apparently. So the question is, am I still practising law? Please kill me now. I'm about as academic as that shit sandwich so no, Lotti, I do not have, nor have I ever had, a fucking law degree. The only bar I have passed is not many, usually, I go in and have a drink.

The phone call is still going. Lotti wants to know how my sister is doing after the horrific car crash that left her teenage son fighting for his life in Arizona. My sister has never set foot in America in her entire life. Pretty much like my father never set foot in America in his whole life. Pretty much like my paternal grandparents never, ever visited America in their entire lives either.

The reason for the question about my sister's child was because apparently Billy "had to go away" for a few months during the marriage. To be there for my sister and to nurse her child back to health. There were complications and the child is permanently disabled so Bill (the angel) had to help get things set up to enable them to get by. Paid for all the medical bills (presumably from the oil wells) and modified the house to make it easier for wheelchair access.

Have I mentioned my sister actually lives in Melbourne and has four healthy children and never set foot in America in her entire life?

The phone call is still going. My grandfather was a high-court judge in Phoenix and she was so sorry to hear of his passing. Mmmmm so was I, but he died up the road in a nursing home and to the best of my knowledge, was a carpenter all his life. Oh, and he never set foot in America. Not once. In all his ninety-two years.

Did I mention my dad reinvents his life when the current

version doesn't work for him any more? Lordy lord, this one is the most creative to date, I think.

The phone call finally ends. There is a God. I just listened mostly, probably because I was in shock and also because I, quite honestly, did not know what to say. I was also torn between protecting Billy and not implicating myself in this latest mess.

One phone call and my life has been repainted. Still wondering why I may have some unresolved childhood issues? Lol.

I go about my life praying that I never hear from Lotti or my father. Ever again. I simply cannot deal with this level of deception. And I am sure as fuck, never putting my hand up to break the bad news to Lotti. Oh no, not me. I'm staying far away from that steaming pile of dung.

Yeah, nice thought. For about a minute anyway.

23
Divorce # 7

It had to happen. Marriage number seven was not turning out to be the fairy tale my dad was hoping for. Surprise.

Months have gone by since that phone call and I had (incorrectly) assumed that Billy had sorted out his shit finally, owned up to the truth and was going to live happily married ever after. Who was I kidding, lol?

I get a call. Yep, you guessed it. It's Lotti and she wants to meet. Please God, no. Just no. I have actually had enough of my dad's shenanigans to last ten lifetimes and I am tired of living in all his different realities. No.

But I'm conditioned to say yes so guess what? I arrange a meeting time. I am such a fucking idiot.

Turns out Lotti is just as lovely in person as she sounded on the phone and looked in her wedding pictures to the devil. She truly is a beautiful soul. My heart instantly goes out to her for believing all the lies that he had fed her.

She brings me flowers and a really nice bottle of wine and we sit down to talk. I am firmly committed to saying very little and simply listening. Please understand that I hate deceit and I hate lies and Billy has put me, yet again, in an untenable position because let's face it, his life is simply a vast web of lies and deceit.

I'm also blown away by the size of the diamond on

Lotti's wedding finger. Let's remember the size of the diamond seems to be determined by the level of deceit or other atrocities Billy has put her through. I also experience a moment of anger at the tens of thousands of dollars I have lost supporting Billy. He bought this particular diamond only about two years after he arrived in London. I wonder if the funds I sent to him contributed to the engagement ring.

I am clearly a chip off the old block because I am furious that I continued to fund him for so many years knowing I would never be reimbursed and also knowing he always lands on his feet. Always. Except when he didn't but I'll get to that.

We open the wine and shoot the breeze for a short while. A very short while. It didn't take long for her to get to the reason for the visit.

Lotti had caught my dad in a lie. I don't remember which one but it was his downfall and Lotti wanted to know exactly whom she had married. I hedged a bit because again, I really did not want to get involved.

She then told me about how my dad had been unemployed for the last few years and she had been propping him up with her money. Until the lie. Then she washed her hands of him. Like me, she doesn't do lies and deceit too well so it was one strike only (I'm sure there were more than one) and Billy was out on his arse.

Then she dropped the bomb.

She was in her late sixties at this time and her late husband's businesses were thriving. Naturally, she wanted her kids to inherit this from her, especially considering the business interests had been their father's. But Billy couldn't really care less about her or her children by this point so he had got himself a sleazebag lawyer and was suing her for millions of dollars. Obviously, he was seeking to fund his sad arse in his unemployment and presumably, retirement.

She was in tears.

I was in tears.

For the love of God Billy, is there no end to your evilness?

They had been married for less than two years.

I caved. There is no way on God's green earth I would let my father do that to her and her kids. It's just wrong. If he had been a wonderful, good, upstanding husband to her, then maybe, but the whole marriage had been built on lies. She married someone else. The guy who nursed his first wife through breast cancer. The guy who raised his tiny children and avoided relationships with women until they were raised. The guy who had never wanted to remarry for the second time until he met her. That saint of a man he had painted himself to be. Yeah, the guy she married was definitely not that guy.

So I followed my moral compass and told her the truth. Every. Last. Bit. Of. The. Real. Billy. My heart broke for this woman. She truly believed all his lies. The look on her face when I told her my mother was still alive. The look on her face when I told her she was actually wife number seven, not two. The look on her face when she heard there were no oil wells. That I wasn't a lawyer. That I was born in Perth, not Phoenix and oh my Lord, the look on her face when she discovered that my sister had never been in Phoenix and none of her children was in a car accident, nor disabled.

That. Look. On. Her. Face.

That day still haunts me as if it was yesterday and it was

more than a decade ago.

Here comes the bomb.

She asked me to write an affidavit with the truth, the whole truth and nothing but the truth. She wanted to take this affidavit to court because her lawyer told her the judge would throw the whole claim out if it could be proven that the marriage was a farce and built on lies. Lies. Lies. Lies.

I felt compelled to do it. How could I not? It was such an emotional day and I knew that I would never sleep again if I rejected her request. She did so not deserve this Billy shit sandwich. Plus, in my book, what he had done to her and was doing to her, was just so terribly wrong. It was despicable really and wrong on so many levels.

Lotti had really loved him and believed all his lies. And for that love, she was going to lose millions of dollars? No. Not if I could help her and her children leave with some sense of decency. Some sense of being able to leave with her head held high and rebuild her life after this one, shocking mistake that we call Billy.

My conscience would not allow me to turn her down. So I wrote the affidavit. She presented it in court. Billy was made aware of who wrote the affidavit.

Lotti got her case thrown out of court.

And the next part of my nightmare began.

24

As in 24-hour police protection

Well, fuck me. The death threats arrived thick and fast and my life turned into a nightmare.

I was frightened for my children, so I sent them to live with their dad until my nightmare with my dad was over. They were still little then, still in primary school and they had and have the best dad ever, so there was no way I was going to expose them to the devil that was my father.

I was forced to watch my back all the time. Billy would appear out of nowhere, following my car, sitting in his car outside my house, outside my office. I was petrified of him and did not trust him to not make good on his threats. His threat was that he was going to slash my face so badly that no man would ever look at me again and maybe, he would just finish the job and put a knife through my heart.

He told me I'd been a snitch when my mother left him and I'd done it again with Lotti. He told me that my guinea pigs' suffering would be nothing compared to what mine would be.

His phone calls were non-stop. He told me that I'd ruined his life. He asked me what evil was inside me that I could not just let him live a happy life. His words hurt so much. I had tried to help him my entire life and was always bailing him out of trouble, but for that, I got no thanks. Ever. I tried to tell him what he had tried to do to Lotti was not right and I had to do the right thing by her. May as well have been talking to a brick wall. He was ropable.

I had hired a private security firm at that point so I had protection around the clock but I eventually had to move homes and go into hiding for a while.

Looking back, I have to laugh. Well fuck me, Billy, I thought it was your responsibility to be a good father. To protect me. What evil was inside me? Really, Dad, you're gonna put that one on me too? There's only one evil bastard between you and me and it ain't me. My conscience is clear and my intentions are always good, despite who raised me.

The sins of the fucking fathers.

I had to get a restraining order on my own father because I truly feared for my life. New low Billy. Father of the fucking year goes to you.

Thankfully after a few months, he gave up and life returned to semi-normal. Haha. Fucking. Ha. What do I know about normal? Lol.

Then the wheel finally turned. I heard that Billy was very, very sick and in awful pain.

And still, he wouldn't phone me and make peace with me. And because I'm an idiot with a really soft heart, I tried to call him many times. Somehow in my own damaged psyche, I figured if he would apologise just once and maybe even tell me he loved me, I'd be able to heal myself.

He wouldn't take my calls. Stubborn old prick. I never spoke to him again and the next time I saw him was at his funeral.

25
Dead Billy

So now that you know what our Billy was like, you'd understand why I loved him so much. Much more than I hated him. He was a larrikin, he was fucking crazy at times and he was a badass. But he was my dad.

The kids and I were driving to Melbourne that December some years ago when I got the call. Billy was dying. He had been battling pancreatic cancer for a year or two and his last days were lived out in incredible pain. He was also very much alone. Seven times divorced and multiple romances in between and during the marriages (he was a serial cheater), and yet he died alone. Says a lot, doesn't it?

We made and received calls many times over the next week. I decided to keep going to Melbourne because it appeared he still had some Billy-fight left in him and wasn't going to go quickly or easily. Plus, the kids and I were looking forward to seeing our friends in Melbourne for Christmas and we were only about 700 kilometres away.

On arriving in Melbourne, I tried to relax with the kids and our friends for a few days but Billy was constantly on my mind. After a few days, I decided the prognosis from various family members was too mixed and I wanted to see Billy for myself.

I established it would cost over two grand to get my car

freighted back to Perth and at the time, I simply could not afford to do this so I booked the kids to fly home four days after I left Melbourne. I had decided, in typical spur-of-the-moment-what- have-I got-to-lose Billy fashion, that I would drive home on my own because I could travel at high speeds as it was only me in the car and I wouldn't be putting my children's lives at risk.

So I loaded up the car and drove. Drove like the fucking wind. I averaged about 200 kilometres per hour most of the way back. It is an almost 4000-kilometre drive to cross the Nullabor and I did it in 37 hours. I *had* to see Billy one last time.

A memory that is very close to my heart is how beautiful the truckies were on that trip home. More on the truckies in a moment. I didn't bother with hotels because there was no time. I snuck a few hours here and there, mostly in the car. Every phone call made me anxious because it seemed that Billy was close to checking out any minute and I was terrified I wouldn't make it back in time to see the little fucker. So when I couldn't keep my eyes open any longer, I stopped at the truck stops along the way and slept for an hour or two before continuing on.

Amazing what state of madness I was in on that journey. Surprised I didn't write myself off. I had a cricket bat in the car as a weapon in case someone attacked me while I slept. Yeah, a cricket bat. Lol. I had so many near-misses driving at 200 kilometres an hour. Complete state of madness I know.

Various family members and friends kept me awake along the way by talking shit to me on the phone for hours, to keep me awake. The rest of the time I listened to my dad's favourite songs by Dean Martin, The Platters, Roy Orbison and sang at the top of my voice to stay awake. I remember belting out 'Only the Lonely' at the top of my voice when the call came.

I was only six fucking hours' drive from the hospital in Fremantle after driving thirty-one hours almost non-stop and he couldn't even wait for me. After all I had done for that man and he couldn't hang on another few hours? Fuck, I was angry. You selfish little fuck.

So, I did what he would have done.

I stopped in the next town. It was Norseman of all places. Same shithole we had spent a year or two living in when I was little. Oh, the irony. Of course, it was fate that I was in that shithole when he died. I bought a bottle of Johnny Walker Black and fifteen packets of Benson & Hedges then drove just out of town and pulled into a truck stop.

I remember sitting on the bonnet of my car slugging straight from the bottle of Johnny Walker, chain-smoking and crying my eyes out. Crying and howling so much I thought I was quite literally going to die too. That's how much the little fucker meant to me.

The incredible kindness of the truckies was literally, amazing. First one, then two came up to ask if I was okay. Do I fucking look okay? I told them my dad had just died with snot rolling down my face and looking like a madwoman. I would have run away from such a wild-eyed, sobbing woman but you know what they did? They circled my car with their trucks so that I couldn't drive off and that they would keep me safe. They told me that once I'd had a good howl and knocked off the whiskey and told some stories to them about my dad, they would stay while I slept to keep me safe. How. Fucking. Good. Are. People.

How fucking fabulous were these guys? I will never ever forget their kindness.

So with a face swollen like a burst arse and the mother (or father lol) of all hangovers, I got on my way the next morning and drove home. I arrived on the evening of New Year's Eve at my empty house. The kids hadn't even left Melbourne yet and my mother, who lives close by could not understand why I was so upset that Billy was dead. I don't blame her for this; he was not kind to her. But hello, he was my dad.

26

The next few weeks were busy and dreadful. The sadness came in waves knowing I would never see Billy again. True to form, he had left his affairs in a mess. There was no will. There were no policies that paid out to set me up for life. You'd think he might have looked after me in death, right? Wrong. Totally unfair. There was a pile of household goods that I had the added chore of having to sell or throw away along with his shitbox of a car. For a man who made and lost many fortunes, Billy had died a pauper.

It was hard packing his clothes because they smelt just like him. Of whiskey and cigarettes and expensive aftershave. I still have a quarter bottle of his favourite aftershave (Aramis) which I sniff from time to time. Like a goddamned junkie. Maybe looking for the nurturing I missed out on in a bottle? Lol. I still have some of his expensive woollen overcoats although they no longer smell like him. Billy had some seriously expensive taste for a poor guy — everything was Armani or Italian wool or Bally leather shoes. Delusions of grandeur right to the end.

I remember trying to pay all his outstanding bills.

I spoke to someone at the gas company who wanted to know when they should cut off the gas. I asked her if she had heard the bit where I said the account holder is dead and she confirmed she had. She then asked me again when I would like to discontinue the service, something like tomorrow or next week. In typical Billy style, I lost it then and screamed at her that he was fucking dead so was probably not going to need to use the gas again. At all. Any more. Never fucking again, so turn the fucking gas off, love. Dead. Men. Do. Not. Use. Gas. Not my proudest moment.

I remember receiving a call from Billy's dentist. Fuck me if he didn't owe her the princely sum of $15000. I enquired what for and she said (and I shit you not), that he had had cosmetic—I repeat *cosmetic* surgery on his teeth 3 months before he died. The dentist told me he wanted to look good when he smiled. Not sure how you look good when you're seventy-three and dying of pancreatic fucking cancer, but then we are talking about Billy. Ever modest, ever charming, still wanting to pull the ladies obviously. The dog. Anyway, the dentist asked me when she could expect payment. And again, I am not proud, but in typical Billy style, I told her that if she was really that fucking stupid to extend credit to a dying man to give him glossy new choppers, then she could go fuck herself. I am a bit embarrassed here, but I also told her which morgue his body was in so that she could go get her fucking teeth back in lieu of payment. Another moment I am not particularly proud of. Grief is a pig. Not proud of myself. At least I never heard from her again. She must have thought I was as crazy as he was. And maybe she would be right!

I then had the absolute joy of opening his laptop so I could access his emails and let the few friends he had, know that he had popped his clogs. No daughter should see what I saw. Ever. FFS!

Nude photos by the dozens of our Billy. Oh boy,

sometimes I wish one could unsee some stuff. The old boy had quite the set of crown jewels. No wonder he never had any issues pulling the girls. That handsome face and that enormous appendage. For a little man, he sure hit the jackpot in that department. Albums of his various wives blowing him and in varying sexual positions or poses. Kill me right fucking now.

I found emails that made me barf in the back of my throat. Billy had built a whole new world on his laptop, in which he was very rich. I know this by the hundreds of photos of some of Perth's finest mansions and finest gardens in suburbs that are well known for being on millionaire's row. Not sure when he had photographed them all but he was claiming them as his very own, showing off how rich he was to all these young Russian girls online. He'd obviously met some of them too because there were photos of him with them. No, I will not go into the different levels of porno in these photos but I will say the girls were barely in their twenties and Billy was well into his seventies at the time. Dirty old bastard. Clearly looking for wife number eight. Un-fucking-believable.

And just so you know what a lovely guy he was, I contacted some of these Russian girls and believe me, they sobbed and sobbed when they heard he had died. I didn't have the heart to tell them they would have fucking sobbed a whole lot more if they'd married the prick and ended up in his real bachelor pad in Perth, which at that stage was a third-floor flat that was about as big as a shoebox.

I'm under no illusions they were crying about the loss of a possible fortune having not managed to snag Billy-the-millionaire and not so much for the loss of Billy the man.

I'm not going to say any more on this subject but, needless to say, I wish I'd never opened that laptop. It was like watching a car accident. You don't want to stare but you are also completely incapable of looking away or simply shutting the laptop. I ended up setting fire to it.

Naturally, it came as no surprise that there was not a single photo of his actual family or his daughters for that matter. No pics of his grandchildren either. What a guy! Family man to the core. Not.

Billy revolved around Billy. Not a nurturing bone in that body but certainly a bone of note lol. Never a truer example of the saying "an erect penis has no conscience", except this penis-holder had no conscience whatsoever.

Epilogue

Anyway, moving right along so I can get rid of the images in my head immediately. Gross. With my typical optimism, I do believe that the life of Billy was survived by many, including me. Yeah, I'm still standing Dad, probably more damaged than most, but still standing. I am rich with memories and poor from all the counselling bills so thanks, Dad.

I've learnt that you don't always get what you want in life but there is no point blaming your upbringing forever. I made the choice to let it go and get on with my life as best I could. I've been mildly successful career-wise and have the best two kids (four really, but that's another book) on the planet, who grew up with a fantastic father and slightly crazy mother, but they seem okay. Thank God. No thanks to Billy (fuck you very much).

Not surprising really that I also learnt many lessons from my dad. I learnt to be compassionate because he was cruel. I learnt to be kind. I learnt to be honest and I hate liars. I learnt to be overly transparent and an open book and I don't create webs of fantasy and lies. I try to live in the real world with all the real-world limitations, ups and downs. My kids tell me I'm a bit of a drama queen but hell! If that's the worst trait I have considering who and what my father was, I'll take it.

He taught me how to be tough and only to rely on myself. My tenacity and never-give-up attitude have stood me in good stead most of the time too. Thanks for that Billy; I could never count on you so I learnt to count on myself.

I learnt that you simply cannot let the sins of the father define who you are. You take on board the lessons, make your own mistakes and successes and carve your own course in life. If you fuck it up, you can only blame yourself. We all have choices. Choose wisely.

Every year on the old bastard's birthday, I pour a Johnny Walker Black or two and think about him. In the early years after he passed, it was with anger and sadness but time goes by and I can now smile at the memories and his non-stop shenanigans. I think about those truckies too and remind myself that people are basically good.

As I have gotten older, I have also come to terms with the fact that my dad was a damaged man long before he became my father. Damaged people damage other people. I respect that he (and all of us) do the best we can with what we know at the time. He tried. His demons were simply stronger than him and the damage was too well ingrained. He simply did his best with what he knew at the time. Just like the rest of us.

Billy always found a way, and I'll bet a pinch of salt to a pound of shit that 10% of him (maybe half of him) is partying hard with the angels and the other 90% is still dancing with the devil dreaming up his next adventure. I'm sure both sides love a pretty boy with a big dick. Who doesn't?!

To all you ladies (and gents) reading this book, if you had a great daddy who loved you to bits and you were the centre of his world, well, fuck you. Just kidding. Sorry, I didn't really mean that. Seriously, you guys were the lucky ones. And I'm very grateful to you for reading my book. Seriously.

The ride goes on.

I miss the old bastard every day.